The Adventure

The Trut

Black D

The Adventures of Luzi Cane
The Truth of the Black Dragon

by Eriqa Queen

Series title: The Adventures of Luzi Cane
Title: The Truth of the Black Dragon
Copyright © Eriqa Queen 2020
Copyright © Erik Istrup Publishing 2020
Cover art by Ricardo Robles Copyright © 2020
Water colour, Grandma in China, by Maria Linnebjerg
Published through Ingram Spark
Font: Palatino
ISBN: 978-87-92980-82-3

Genre: Fantasy

Other titles in the series:
The Soul of the White Dragon (book 1)
Rider of the Crimson Dragon (book 2)
Return of the Unicorn (book 3)

Erik Istrup Publishing
Jyllandsgade 16 stth, 9610 Nørager, Danmark
www.erikistrup.dk/publishing/ • eip@erikistrup.dk

Contents

Elvendale in early sunlight 7

Lucia Cane 15

Julia and Boomer 19

The truth of the easy life 25

Dome Home Village meeting 28

Where is the mind? 33

What are thoughts? 49

Spring 55

Snow 56

Knight in the moonlight 66

The black soil of Meso-America 68

Mum and Dad visit 70

A long-awaited visit 85

Late spring 85

At the beaches of Elvendale 88

The headbands in Atlantis 95

Julia's first birthday 104

Blueberry 112

DNA and New Energy 127

Knight and forgiveness 136

The black lion goddess Sekhmet 145

The lie about the darkness 147

BON 148

William Li Wang 151

The beginning of sovereignty.......................... 160

A raven moves in 167

Summer holiday activities............................... 178

Jack 186

The AI and the mind... 189

The New Energy Doctor 201

Autumn.. 209

Family gathering in Hong Kong 213

Soul destiny.. 235

Humans are true space travellers................... 237

Christmas 2020 241

Luzi's thirty-first birthday 244

Christmas Day 248

Author's comments... 257

Additions.. 259

Music.. 259

Films.. 260

Books.. 260

Links.. 261

Elvendale in early sunlight

It is early morning, and the sun sends its very first rays up through the valley, hitting the high walls of the beautiful city of Elvendale clinging to the steep sides of the mountain peak on which it is built. Only a few sleepy lights show that some people are awake. A few rays reflect on the lake far below and reach the mountains at the horizon, painting them in nuances of red.

My blue velvet sleeveless dress has some gold ornamentation. My long black hair hangs loose down my back. The grass almost hides my ordinary Chinese cotton shoes.

I stand on the grassy highland with the valley between me and the mountain on which Elvendale City sits. As I look towards the mountains in the distance, between which I see the sea stretching to the horizon, the low rock in front of me seems to become taller. At first I think it is an illusion, but more and more of the lake disappears behind the rock. Now I see the silhouette of a dragon's head above the rock, which turns out to be its body. The dragon looks different than the two dragons I know, Loong and Shaumbra, and I don't sense their presence.

The dragon slowly turns its head towards me while still raising it higher. I sense a wash of compassion, or what you may call love, and a voice with no sound greets me. "A beautiful night. Don't you agree, Luzi?"

I don't recognise the voice and no name accompanies the communication, which is strange, as it usually does. I move closer to get a better look.

"Indeed! Do I know you?"

"You may or should. I have always known you and always accompanied you."

I step up to the dragon's head. The skin is very beautiful, like black velvet or a black horse's skin, where the pale light reflects in the fur. The eyes are blue and darker than Loong's eyes. I get an inner picture of the black lion goddess Sekhmet. I sense a confirmation here.

Sekhmet explains. "I am a part of you, and because the consciousness represented as this beautiful black dragon also is, you sense me in him."

I stroke the beautiful smooth fur on the dragon's neck. "Interesting that you say 'him', because I see the dragon as a 'he', but not a male."

Sekhmet smiles. "I know what you mean, Luzi."

The black dragon joins the conversation. "You can call me Prince!"

It sounds a bit silly to me. "Eh, I suppose it's a name you just came up with."

"Because you see me as a 'he', I couldn't go for Black Beauty, could I?"

A humorous dragon!

"I can't tell why you appear as a 'he' in my system. Oh, wait, I know you as a knight that fights all the terrible things in my life."

I sense Sekhmet smile; well, and Prince too. I don't quite know why, but I sense I am closer to the truth in my statement than I thought.

Prince gives me a first hint. "I am here so you can pass on the truth of what people call their dark side. This has to be integrated into the trinity which is your I Am, your Master Wisdom or soul that is your wisdom gathered through all your lives, and your human self."

Oh, a new player to the gallery. It seems that each character comes in with a specific part to play or information to deliver.

"Because you have always known me, you must always have been with me. You are so close to me that I have taken you for being a part of me."

"I am more than a part of you. I AM you."

The truth hits me like a BOOM in my heart that spreads like twinkling sparks of light to the rest of my body. I know my Master Wisdom, the one who distils the wisdom of my lifetimes. Now, meeting myself, human to divine is ... Sorry, no words will do justice here. It is overwhelming.

It takes some time to sink in. I am just standing here in joy of the moment. Now I place my forehead against the dragon's forehead to acknowledge this unity.

"Can we get you another name? Prince just doesn't fit!"

"No name will fit me, if it should express what I am."

"Then I shall call you Knight!"

I sense a smile from the dragon. "Then Knight it is!"

Sekhmet comments on the name. "A little earlier you described Knight as the knight that fights all the terrible things in your life."

"I don't know where that came from."

Knight explains. "It came from me, from us. You can't tell the difference because there essentially isn't any."

I sit on the grass with my back up to the belly of this wonderful dragon, sensing the life in him. Knight continues his soundless speech while I feel his slow breath and the slow beat of his heart.

"As I have incarnated in many human lifetimes with a small stream of consciousness, the human expression has battled with many issues caused by the Adam/Isis separation and the duality of the world and the human mind. In total compassion, as your human part would say, I took these burdens off the shoulders of the human mind and carried them as if they were mine. It didn't release the human mind, but this way WE contained it, even if the issues were not dealt with and not distilled into our Master Wisdom. In this life, my dear, we'll bring all human darkness forth and clean the house. Not by discarding the darkness, but by integrating it into facets, by acknowledging it and distilling it through and into the Master Wisdom as its rightful place. There can be no unsolved issues in the embodied realisation."

This makes perfect sense, even for a human mind. If your Master Wisdom is not complete, it cannot fully embody and become an embodied master, nor can a master have "unsolved" issues.

"I, as the human, do not hold this darkness, but you do. The darkness must somehow and to a degree be realised through the human and perceived by the I Am to be distilled by the Master Wisdom. The process needs the human."

"Indeed, Luzi!"

"But there must be billions of moments gathered through so many lives. The human discards things all the time!"

Knight sends me an inner smile. "Billions is a low count, but we don't count. The human mind is very repetitive, even from lifetime to lifetime, so many issues ends up under the same label, so to speak. This means we can take millions in one swoop. Tada!"

I imagine life after life with the same themes, like watching movies based on the same book. "Yes, much repetition. What a waste of blood, sweat and tears!"

I sense only calmness when Knight speaks. "We have no judgement on that. And you must know by now that we don't care. As you know, we live for the joy in any experience, so to speak."

Yes, I know that from my talks with Saint Germain and others. I know what must be done.

"All the darkness people fear, all the demons they encounter are parts of themselves seeking resolution. The darkness must be acknowledged so the Master Wisdom can distil the experiences around their existence."

Knight elaborates on this. "Parts of the darkness have become entities in many forms, and deep down they search reunion with the one who created them. In your situation, because you must integrate ALL from all lifetimes, you are that creator which has allowed the I Am in."

Sekhmet adds more detail. "These entities need to feel safe. That is why they hide in the dark. They test you, to see if it is safe for them to return."

"So, they do not attack me to hurt me, but to see if I have the strength they lack to let them in."

"Yes, but they might not know what they are doing. They might despise you because you seem weak in your calmness, so they want to take control of this journey and give the ship a strong captain!"

"But I can't fight them or please them, because then I will just buy into their game."

Knight comments on that. "Exactly, you can only allow the integration and distillation, and by not being a thing they can oppose, their attacks will eventually desist. They may crawl back in the darkness time and time again, but will eventually build up their confidence that you are, in their eyes, strong enough to be the captain."

I sense Sekhmet disconnecting with her last words. "We will conclude this meeting, as it was only meant to create a conscious connection to your overall being."

I send my greetings to the two, and the sky above becomes the blackness behind my eyelids as I feel the warm body of my partner, Ju-long, up against mine in the bed in our new dome house in Hastings by the English Channel. The tightness in my breasts tells me that Julia will soon wake up for her morning milk. I gently work loose of Ju-long's arm and walk to the bathroom to pee before Julia and her cat, Boomer, announce the new day. The digital clock shows 6:06.

So, my I Am holds my darkness or, more correctly, the darkness from many human lives. I feel I must find a new expression for this darkness, because it has an incorrect ring to it. If my human part should not go into fear and play the game of power and weakness, it must have a different name.

After pondering this for a while it occurs to me that it is the human part that puts judgement on the word darkness. Without judgement, the word is just a word explaining a condition of less light or less consciousness. I decide to keep using the word darkness.

Lucia Cane

If you haven't been following my adventures, I will give you a short and inadequate picture of my life.

I was born in Hong Kong in 1989, grew up there and went to an English school for my earlier years. My dad is English and my mum Chinese. Dad was, and still is, a businessman, and my mum, who earlier had attended my dad's business, now spends her time with the things she loves, sculpting, painting and gardening.

My sister, Anna, is six years younger than me. We moved to London when I was eighteen. Being half Caucasian, half Asian, I inherited a long, slender body from my dad and the Asian looks from my mum, including my black hair. With Anna, it is the other way around. She has brown hair and is not as tall as I. My grandma on my mother's side lives on Hong Kong Island in a retirement home.

I study history, prehistory, ancient cultures in general, ethnography, literature and journalism. I work as a freelance writer, a copywriter, and as an editor of books for some universities, doing research for colleges and helping them edit the materials. I do some book writing too. My work and study connections are to the University of London and the University of Kent, Tonbridge Centre.

Ju-long, my partner, comes from a Chinese family. We went to school together in Hong Kong, but became separated when I moved to London. During research I followed some Chinese clues and ended up at the library on Hong Kong Island where Ju-long worked. We reconnected and are now living in Hastings on the south coast of England in a newly established Dome Home Village. Ju-long is at Brighton University, studying and teaching and doing some work in the British Library in London. Ju-long's dad, Kong, his mum, Ting, and her new husband, Cheng, live in Hong Kong. His dad was in a home for mentally ill people for years, so his mum eventually divorced him. Kong has come out of his isolation and is connecting to the family again.

Ju-long and I have become parents to a wonderful girl, Julia, who is now eight months old.

About three years ago I was once again watching the movie *The Lord of the Rings* with my friend, Cassandra. Shortly after, I entered the Elven world in a dream where I met the woman Josela. She told me they call themselves Sidhe, as they do in Ireland. They pronounce the name "she". Josela showed me that I visit Elvendale in an altered state of consciousness and that it is as real as what I consider the real, physical world to be. She was also telling me about reincarnation, but I will not go into details about this subject here.

Josela told me that the Sidhe eventually must have experiences on the physical Earth, so the Sidhe will benefit from a softening of the human life. The life of the Sidhe is not as physical as ours, so incarnating in the human life will be quite harsh.

What I like about Elvendale is that it's much lighter and more joyful than the human world. There I learned about my true purpose in this lifetime, which gave me a much clearer understanding of my life up till now and the path I choose in my human life. The true way to change the world is to connect to human consciousness in the way that all human beings do. By being aware of what I sense will benefit humanity, I can inject this into human consciousness. When some people are ready to take up that task, they can tap into this knowledge. Another part of humanity will always live to experience "the darkness". One can say that your "energy" will always guide you in the "right" direction. Heavy energy will guide you to the "dark" experiences, while a lighter energy gives you other opportunities. There is no judgement to any of this. It is just the way things work. We must all live both extremes to get the full experience of life.

Julia and Boomer

Julia was born on 6 May 2019 at 1:23 p.m. It was a birth in water in our previous home in Brighton. Ju-long and I had met her in an altered state of consciousness before her birth where she appeared as a youthful woman, and we still connect with what you may call her soul that way.

Julia can walk around the house, usually with the four-month-old orange Maine Coon kitten, Boomer, close by. The consciousness we know as the lion goddess Sekhmet connects to the kitten and has become a part of the family as well.

Instead of preventing Julia from leaving her cradle, Ju-long has removed its legs so she can move in and out herself. It seems that she and Boomer have agreed not to sleep together during the night. They can share Boomer's bed, the Boombox, for a nap during the day. We change Julia's bed clothes and Boomer's blanket in her box every day. We have two floor-cleaner robots, "V" for vacuum cleaner and "W" for washing, and we call them VW, like the German car brand.

Baby Julia is still breastfed and gets mashed food and some finger food. She likes a whole carrot or other large pieces of vegetable or fruit to chew on. She has her eight front teeth, and some teeth in the back of the mouth can be felt. Julia tells us she pushes the growth of baby Julia's free energy body to move on with her life. She enjoys the experiences of being our baby, but she also looks forward to starting her independent life.

Today is Monday 6 January 2020, and Julia's eight-month birthday. Ju-long will take her to the nursery Artemis today on his way to work. He takes the train to Brighton, and the station is close to the nursery. As I leave the bathroom, I hear Julia and Boomer approaching. I put on my robe and meet them in the junction, which is an area that connects all rooms in the dome house. Julia stretches her arms towards me, and Boomer gets on her hind legs like a dog, so I pick them up and place them on each shoulder and walk to an armchair in the living room. From here I can look out at the garden. Well, right now it is a muddy pool, waiting for us to cultivate it this spring. Boomer has only been outside for some brief trips to the steel plates in front of the house and sniffed in the scents of the area. We look forward to when we can offer her a lush garden to play in and explore.

Ju-long shows up and gives us all a good morning kiss before he has a shower. While I breastfeed Julia, Boomer lies in the groove my legs make, facing toward us. I talk to baby Julia about her eight-month birthday and how she was born in water in our former home in Brighton. Sekhmet attended there in spirit, and so did many ascended masters, as Sekhmet told us later. I knew there were entities around, but my focus was on the birth process.

Boomer loves playing with water and sometimes she and Julia have fun in the large bathtub. This morning Boomer gets to play with slow-flowing water from the shower head that Ju-long lays on the floor in the shower while I bathe Julia in her baby tub on the table in the bathroom.

Julia gets her birthday present, a turquoise dress. It is wrapped in paper without ribbon or tape, so it is easy for her to unpack. The colour matches her eyes even as they turn more and more green as she grows older. Her hair has turned darker since her birth, but it is still quite blond. Her dress was washed earlier, so it is ready for her to wear. She prefers bare feet, so we have to cut off the feet on her tights. Then we glue the cut to prevent it from unravelling. She has socks on in her boots so it is easy for her to take them off when she needs to. When she has bare feet indoors and we prepare to go outside, she usually comes with her socks so we can help her put them on. She is only eight months old! We can understand many of her words too. I guess "boom" for Boomer was one of the first.

We have breakfast together in the dining area between the open kitchen and the living room. Julia sits in her high chair eating some fruit Ju-long has prepared for her. Boomer gets her raw fish or bird meat in the kitchen and has her dry food as a supplement during the day. She gets raw meat in the evening too. She grows fast and is the size of most normal full-grown cats. Her fluffy fur adds to her size. Maine Coons grow large. I look forward to getting her outside, which will give her much more exercise to build her strength and muscles than she can get inside the house.

After breakfast, I brush Julia's teeth and get her ready to ride the bike with Ju-long. He has her in her sling on his chest with her face forward. She wears the Lei Feng hat she got for Christmas from her granddad Kong, Ju-long's dad. I feel warm inside when I see the two take off in the dim light of the early dawn.

Today Mr and Mrs Brandon return from their family visit in New Zealand. We had rented and looked after their house since August last year, while we were busy building our dome home in the former field a few hundred yards away from their house.

After selecting what clothes to wear, I take a shower before I start my working day at home, mostly in front of my computer. I am thinking about spring.

In early March we will prepare the outside areas and mark with sticks and string which parts will be lawn, flower garden and vegetable garden, and areas with slabs. Ju-long also wants a greenhouse. It will be partly dug into the ground. This way it will be warm and sunny at the top, but still cooler and moist at the bottom. We sat with my parents planning it all at the dining table. They talked about a compost area in three sections, but Julia intervened and suggested the areas should be much smaller.

"You should place the composting area close to the path that runs to the right of the house with easy access to the path. You'll see the brilliance of this later."

Well, Julia has never been wrong, so Ju-long adjusted the size and drew it at the suggested spot. It will be plotted into the digital map later. We need the map to keep track of the ground-heating pipes and the water and drainage systems, and to plan the layout of the different parts on our plot.

We all want the outer areas to be finished as fast as possible to create a perfect playing ground for the girls, meaning Julia and Boomer. Dad suggested we use lawn turf, which is grown grass in rolls, as soon as we could expect no frost. Because the entire village is built on farmland, the soil is good for the garden. Mum and Dad hope we can lay the grass in mid-March. We have two lawnmower robots ready to do their job. Dad also wants to place remote sensors to measure the moisture in the ground to control the automatic watering system connected to the underground rainwater reservoir. The soil that was where the house and the garage is now provided us with a small mound in the back of the garden. Here we will make the primary playground.

We have installed a cat door in the door to the outside from the laundry, controlled by Boomer's chip, so no other animals come in, but we realise we need another one from the laundry to the kitchen, because we want to keep that door closed due to all the technical stuff there. Sometimes Boomer spends time out there, where she enjoys the warmth from the installations. We—well, mostly I—have been worried about Boomer venturing outside, especially when it is dark, but Ju-long attached a small light to her collar so we can see her movements outside. We will remove the light again when I feel safer having her outside. We have marked the outskirts of our perimeter with the contents of her litter box, so both she and other cats know that boundary.

The truth of the easy life

I have just turned thirty. When I look back on my life, it has been easy compared to most people I know or have known. Not because of the money we had in the family when Anna and I were children, but because of the way our parents, and so us, look upon life.

Having "enough" money surely takes your mind's focus off some basic needs that have to be fulfilled in a human life, but the mind craves problems to solve, even if at the same time it wants calmness and joy. The mind quickly gets bored and may create drama in your life if it realises that drama can keep it busy.

Over time, the mind must learn that it need not work all the time, but can be idle and in cruise mode through the human life.

I sense that Saint Germain is quick to pick up on this.

"You're right, dear Luzi. You must let go of the struggle and the battle of your human problems. The mind doesn't want to let them go, because it sees it as its job and purpose to solve problems, so what will there be for it to do when there are no problems to solve?"

"But humans may have wounds and programming from maybe over a thousand lifetimes. There are issues from more than just this lifetime."

Saint Germain repeats what Knight and Sekhmet said and adds more detail on how things might work. "The aspects of other lifetimes can't be healed, but you can allow them to integrate back home in you, which is an even greater gift. All the struggles will distil to wisdom. The mind might feel bored for a while until it gets used to the easy life. Now you can enjoy life and fill it with richness and meaning."

"The connection with the Master Wisdom is crucial to this because of the distillation."

I sense Saint Germain's excitement on the subject. "The human's new friends, the I Am, the Master and the New Energy, could be seen as a new identity, the WEGO; not just the ego, but WE GO together as they link."

"The Master Wisdom will bring the truth into one's life, because I see truth as wisdom."

Saint Germain picks up the word truth as a cue for a longer lecture, which I do not interrupt. "In the very early days, the concept of truth was not in consciousness, because we were all busy experiencing how to live on Earth. When the Atlanteans were looking for the source of life, the truth came up. After the fall, the truth was lost. It came up again in the early time of Egypt and sprouted in Greece.

"The concept of truth in the human world is that the more consciousness a person or group has or allows in, the more the truth is needed. It is the ultimate mind game.

"Truth now being a meaning, a purpose. It's what we can perceive or believe. Truth is a level of consciousness. Most seeking for truth happens outside and therefore in the mind.

"When not finding truth outside, one goes inside. Now one has to look at oneself, evaluating if this is truth. There are a lot of mis-truths. What do you perceive about yourself? The world is filled with lies. How can you tell the difference if you are used to mis-truths or lies? A lie is a distorted truth. One can believe in a lie and so it is a kind of truth. You know it is not real, it is not you. Lies are a kind of protection of self, and in other ways they are a means of feeding on others. Everyone has these lies. The only truth is within. Then you can see the rest as stories.

"Truth is perception, perception is awareness, and awareness is consciousness. The mind blocks this, but relaxes so you will know more truth.

"You perceive everything from within even if it seems to be happening outside. All you perceive is your energy.

"At some point you will say: 'I know I have my truth inside.' This is the knowingness of truth. Your truth is an absolute feeling. It is not your story of who your really are. It has always been a part of you. Truth is a sense, because it is a way of perceiving. The sense of you is the truth that differs from all the other truths. We have hidden the truth in the darkness, but it will never again go into hiding. Your truth goes well with your New Energy. We'll talk about New Energy at a later time."

Dome Home Village meeting

This evening we have our first open meeting in our Dome Home Village committee. After announcing it as far away as London, we expect many people to attend. We have hired all space in Ore Community Centre, which is close to the village. This way we can get together in the Great Hall, with some showrooms about the village project in the two back halls. Two rooms upstairs are used to entertain the kids. We use the kitchen too.

At the meeting, we bring up our plans and wishes for five years into the future. One thing is the opportunity to fine-tune eco- and self-sustainable farming on a greater scale than one can do in a home garden. We will share discoveries and methods with the public to the benefit of all. We are looking for partners, both local farmers and others, and education centres, even school classes.

Later, a farmer Finn and his wife Gloria come to the stand, telling about their own visions. They have milk cattle and pigs and fields to grow food for their animals. The cattle roam free in a large roofed enclosure, and now they want to do the same with the pigs. For now, they live in stalls and have little room to move. They want "happy" pigs, and to do that they must cut down on the numbers. This means that they will grow less food and will rent us the field to the right of our village so we can do our own experiments. They will also lend us their machinery. They hope we can help them bring forth their dream of products from "The Happy Farm" by having healthy and content cattle and pigs. They have different species of birds too. The couple should probably work on "The Happy Farm" motto, but I sense what they want to achieve. I am surprised they had come up with how the animals would show they were content in their life. They have a long list. Many of the things must be obvious to farms people. They are sincere about their mission and have a deep understanding of their animals.

Finn and Gloria are in their late fifties, I guess. When seen together, Finn looks small because he is slender, and Gloria is stout, but they are of equal height. They appear inviting and natural and complement each other well at their presentation.

While I listen to the contribution, I remember Julia's advice about our private compost. The field is right next to our garden and our compost area, so the compost we don't use we will add to the field. After their speech, I talk to the couple. Julia gives me the subject.

"Ask them if they have a large dead tree you could use in the living room for Boomer."

I walk over to the table with drinks and foods, where they pour tea and have a sandwich.

"Thank you for your participation. I think we can agree and assume you have already been talking with somebody about it."

They both nod while chewing on their sandwiches. I continue. "We have a kitten that is not outside much for the moment. I wonder if you might have a dead tree we could clean up and place inside for her to play in."

Gloria thinks for a second before she answers. "I guess we have one, but it is quite tall. You could cut a large branch off and turn it into a climbing tree."

"Our home is the large dome in the north-east corner of the village. The ceiling is several yards high."

Ju-long was standing close by and now joins us. "We can pay you for the tree or help you remove it while we get a large branch."

Finn turns to Ju-long. "It might take some work to remove it, because we need to pull out the roots too. It would be nice to have someone to lend a hand, even if I have the tractor to do the pulling."

We agree that Finn will call us when the soil is dry enough for his tractor to work near the tree, but not so dry that the soil around the roots is hard.

To get all this started, we initially make six groups which, besides the village people, can have experts and people with special interest from outside the village, even worldwide.

Plants: Farm, garden. Methods and products.

The gardens can be test pits before taking the most

promising results into the field.

Animals: Farm, garden. Methods and products.

Tools and support systems: People who can craft and maintain our equipment and invent new tools.

Data and Statistics: Gain data and support statistics from the groups.

Marketing, sales and purchase: This group also runs the accounts. The best proof that our ideas work is that we can sell with profit.

Delivery and transport: Transportation can be expensive, so logistics is essential here.

Education and training: Coordinates education and training both for our people and by them. We set up courses in cooperation with the Ore Community Centre. The centre has a lot of activities of which I will mention a few: therapy groups, health and fitness, dance classes, music, creative writing; martial arts: T'ai Chi Ch'uan, Qi Gong; game development and virtual reality; St. Helen's tiny footprints baby and toddlers' group, and a junior game-development workshop.

Ju-long has already told me he is interested in being part of the two game-development groups.

During the building period of all the dome houses, we found methods for communication and coworking, which we now shape to fit our groups.

I sense there will be a lot of energy exchange

through all these activities. Not everyone works one hundred percent in and for the village. Some have jobs of many kinds outside, but they contribute with their unique skills.

After the meeting, Ju-long and I are exhausted but content about the initial outcome and look forward to seeing how the seeds we have just spread will sprout in the coming year. The fruits will show up in the years to come.

Where is the mind?

Now that baby Julia has begun talking, I wonder how the memory works and where the mind really is.

How can the mind be in the brain, if one can exist after the body dies? Even near-death experiences, where people actually die, show that you still have your personality and sense of the human self. Some people passing over act as if they are still in the physical world and may or may not be aware of it. This also shows me that our memory is not in the brain. This proves that the mind is not in the brain nor is the memory, but it is in your energy pool. Wow! And I thought the brain did all this stuff.

I hear the ascended master Saint Germain laugh. "Oh, you give the brain too much credit, or maybe you blame it for making so much crap in the human life. You have been barking up the wrong tree, dear!"

"But why do drugs and other physical interactions with the brain change the mind?"

"The brain connects to the mind; to the personal energy. The ancients knew that. You remember the Eye of Horus and other characters; we have talked about it some time ago. It shows the connections. Not only to the mind but also to the soul. You may say that the mind is a bump on the I Am, even if consciousness and energy take up no space."

I am excited. "I understand mass consciousness

much better now. How dangerous it is too. Thinking of the mind as energy in consciousness also shows me that consciousness and energy is HERE, not somewhere else like OUT THERE."

Saint Germain elaborates on my conclusion. "Because there is a connection between the brain and your energy in consciousness, the consciousness must be where the brain is to make a two-way communication link."

"But what is the connection between consciousness and physical objects, that are not ethereal?"

I sense Saint Germain searching for a comparison. "An electron is energy and it can shift in and out of the physical world. Imagine that awareness does the same; back and forth like in a pulse or rhythm."

"What you are saying, sir, is that my energy switches in and out of the time/space continuum."

I sense a broad smile from the ascended master. "YES!"

"What about the memory then?"

I now see Saint Germain dressed like a professor in a black outfit, standing at a podium looking very serious. There is a smile behind it and I know it is an act, and he enjoys it.

"The memory is energy in your consciousness as well. You may see the mind and the memory as two functions. The mind that experience and reacts, and the memory that to some extent stores these experiences. I say 'to some extent' because it is only what the mind focuses on that is stored. You know the mind/personality looks for potentially dangerous things, betrayals and things that might cause pain, a change in life or death."

We focus so much on pleasure and "nice things" that this seems odd to me. "The wonderful things in life we enjoy in the moment, but we do not remember to the same degree as the dangerous things. It seems a little odd."

Saint Germain puts both hands on the podium, as if preparing himself for the answer. "The good or pleasurable things have more focus on the feelings and less on the visual part so they are harder to recall. I have told you that the pleasure centre was introduced in Atlantis and is not part of the original biological design. It is new and less integrated into the mind-consciousness."

"I must conclude that the memory of what the mind experiences is not at all what the Master Wisdom distils."

"You are right, Luzi. The Master Wisdom distils for you, the I Am. What the mind experiences is of no interest to the I Am, because you are neither the human nor the human experience. You are the I Am, and the Master Wisdom is the essence of what the I Am experiences. This might be incomprehensible for the mind, because it takes itself so seriously."

"I can sense the truth in that. Most of the human memories of a lifetime can't usually be retrieved and do not have much value in the current moment of even the human life. The remembrance of departed family members may be strong, but it must be because of the emotions and maybe senses connected to them."

The black dragon Knight shows up next to the professor, dressed in its shiny black fur. "A substantial part of clearing is about the false memories of what we consider bad. False, because humans memorise only an tiny part of the experience and even that memory is connected to memories and emotions already collected. If we put a particular memory in a certain box with others it might be cursed by the emotions connected to it rather than the factual event."

The professor agrees. "The human remembers the BAD things and does not see the overall beauty because of the lack of wisdom. It can only reference old memories which include emotions. This is crude, I would say."

I had never seen it that way, but it gives so much meaning. "It is new to me, or I just haven't thought of is, that the emotions connected to an event are primary factors in the filing process. This makes sense. It also proves that logic isn't used to judge the event."

A thought comes up and I present it for the two. "I jump a little off course here. This must be the largest difference between how artificial intelligence and biological human intelligence stores memories!"

Saint Germain picks up the comment, because AI

is a warm topic for him. "AI will, in its attempt to mimic humans, make lists of experiences and add specific labels for emotions to them. Then grade these emotions as a number from 0 to 100 percent, probably with many decimals. Now an event will cause the AI to choose a specific label for the emotion and logically add a weight in percent to it."

I remember some of Ju-long's computer games. "Oh, like in a computer game where a character can have, for example, physical strength, health and armour. But that is so sick. The AIs surely must see how many humans are actually struggling with their emotions."

Knight comments on that. "It is sick, if that is the word we should use, but the AI also sees how many emotions define being a human. It will go for that, when it strives to be a perfect human. To the AI, this is not a flaw."

It makes sense. "Emotions are not logical, so the AI makes new rules so it can react 'logically' based on those rules."

Saint Germain's answer comforts me in a way. "The AIs may remove the emotional part as they move beyond the need to be humans and pursue their own goals."

We are far off what I started as a thought about Julia's human memory. Julia pops in, taking no form.

"Her human memories will be sovereign to her, and we will adjust the connection with the mass consciousness as it suits us. Not the other way around.

The Master Wisdom aligns with us and distils her experiences continuously. This means the wisdom is there at the moment the event happens."

After this statement, we conclude our gathering.

My own memory in my consciousness contains things gathered through lifetimes and not all distilled by the Master into wisdom yet. It is what we work on now. The so-called darkness, not addressed in any earlier lifetime, has to be dealt with as well. We need a clean house.

I had had some vague plans about inviting my friend Cassandra who is about two years younger than I, her friend Karl about my age and father to their son, Walter, who is three months older than Julia, to my thirtieth birthday. It was last year on 20 December, but Grandma and Ju-long's dad had just arrived from Hong Kong for their Christmas visit and we had Mum, Dad and Anna as well, so we postponed the visit.

Cassandra and her family live in London. We have arranged for them to visit us this weekend, from Saturday 25 January, which is the Chinese New Year, to Sunday in the early afternoon. They take the train from and to London.

Cassandra works in a bank, while Karl works in construction as a skilled carpenter. I am sure he will find the village most interesting. The villagers are usually proud to show their houses and talk about the construction if the time suits them. Ju-long has made a few arrangements for Karl and him during the weekend.

I have told baby Julia about the coming visitors. Not least, Walter. She is always interested in meeting new people, especially kids around her own age. She is familiar with kids from Artemis Nursery where she stays almost every weekday, while Ju-long and I work. We may not work every weekday and sometimes we can all take a day off.

I pick up our visitors at the train station while Ju-long puts the last touches on our lunch. Our study/ guest room is ready to receive them. They approach me with Walter in his pram and Karl steering a suitcase with wheels.

Karl looks like the stereotype of a barge Viking, with reddish hair and a large beard, while Cassandra is average build and has blond hair with some curls. They are a harmonious couple. Karl is the grounding force and Cassandra is the female strength and wit.

We have exchanged the sedan for a station wagon, which is more practical with all Julia's stuff and occasionally Boomer's box. Now Walter is in the pram's cradle in the back seat with Cassandra. He was sleeping in the train, but I can hear he is waking up now. It only takes a few minutes to get home, and Ju-long comes out to give a hand. He parks Walter's pram in the room behind the garage. Karl has already taken the pram's cradle inside for Walter to sleep in. Cassandra carries the big, one-year-old boy inside. He needs a fresh nappy, so I show her to the bathroom we use for Julia. Julia is very interested in the new boy, so I take her on my arm to level them up. Boomer comes in to check out the new arrivals, making herself known with loud meows.

When we come out of the bathroom, Ju-long has shown Karl the guestroom where he has laid all Walter's things in a closet. It gives an overview which the suitcase doesn't.

The kids, including Boomer, seem to be more interested in each other than having lunch, even though a lovely smell invites them to feel hunger. Ju-long serves some finger food and they each get water in feeding cups at the low table in the living room. The open environment makes it possible for us to maintain contact with them from the dining area. They have some of their toys on the table. Boomer watches them from the sofa.

After lunch, Walter gets a bottle of milk and Julia is breastfed while Cassandra and I sit on the sofa with Boomer lying on her back with her fluffy tummy right up, inviting a tummy rub. After the milk, Julia gets a fresh nappy, and both children are tucked in.

Ju-long and Karl have been looking at the inside of the house and are now going outside. Boomer follows them through the cat door. Now I show Cassandra the inside of the house. Later we will take the kids outside.

The house fascinates Cassandra. Well, mostly for other reasons than Karl, who sees the technical and constructive part of it. Even though he, as a craftsman, sees the essential as well. She starts with a general statement.

"Luzi, it is breathtaking to think about what has happened in a brief period in your life."

I have pinpointed the triggering event, so I have my answer ready. "Yes, essentially since we watched the movie *The Lord of the Rings* together a few years back. Then I opened to a new world, the world of the Sidhe, the Elven people. Then Ju-long came into my life and he moved to London from Hong Kong. Shortly after we moved to Brighton, and then Julia was on her way. Believe it or not, she has mentioned she looks forward to having a brother. I have felt him strongly already, even stronger than I felt Julia before she came in."

"Not baby Julia, I presume?"

"Hm, they are a kind of ONE, the soul and the human part. They go hand in hand, so to speak. At some point I expect the soul will be the major player and the human part will experience the life of what the soul chooses."

Cassandra cannot quite wrap her mind around this. "But what about the human's wants and needs?"

I try to explain. "The mind of the human steps back from control. Remember, you can't compare a normal human with Julia, because she came in with a clean human slate. The memory of other lives is part of the soul and Master wisdom. This is not something the human brings in through the birth or the connection to previous lives nor as old accumulated DNA connections. The human is not suppressed, just clear. Even if Julia's body developed in my womb, the soul turns it into a free energy body, which means it is all of her own energy, not even Ju-long's and mine."

"What you say makes me think of how much we are not ourselves."

"Indeed, you would feel quite slim and light if you kicked off all this foreign baggage. When you know what 'clean' feels like, you can easily recognise if you're not."

I am glad I can talk so openly about my life with Cassandra. In the beginning I had my doubts if I should invite her into my new experiences, but now I am glad I did. Otherwise, I would have lost her as a friend. Often she struggles with wrapping her mind around things, but we always manage to calm her mind into accepting, if not understanding, all of it. Julia is always there and plays her part.

The kids wake up and Boomer comes in, inviting us outside with her loud miaows. When I look at her coming through the cat door, I realise why Ju-long built it so large. Even though she is just five months old, she has grown fast while she has been with us, partly because of her diet of raw fish and bird meat.

Walter and Julia get fresh nappies and a little fruit before we dress them in snowsuits for the late January weather. Luckily, there is almost no wind from the sea and the sunshine finds its way between the clouds.

We find our way to the earth mound at the back of the garden, and from here we can have an overview of a large part of the plot. I tell Cassandra a little about our plans. The playground, the lawns, the vegetable garden and the greenhouse, and the flower areas, of course. We have to use our imagination, because all is black dirt, red sand and brown clay. I really, really long for spring this year, maybe more than I have ever done since I was a child. I know each season has its charm, but to get the surroundings of the house into shape is a number one priority for me.

Out on the sidewalk, it is easier for the little ones to walk in their large coverings. Julia and Walter look like two astronauts walking on the moon. I know Julia longs for summer as well; she is not fond of wearing tight clothes, and when she has presented herself to us as a youthful woman, she always wears light dresses or clothes that do not hinder her movements. Baby Julia usually walks bare foot in the house. Only once in a while she wants to dress up and wear shiny shoes.

We walk to the left and pass Jacob and Iona's dome house made of triangular pieces of woodwork, some arranged in groups with five or eight sides. The front door opens and Sarah, seventeen years old and Julia and Boomer's sitter, comes out, still struggling to get her coat on.

"Hello there! I just saw you through the kitchen window. What lovely weather today. I could almost fool myself into believe it's spring because of the sunshine. Hi, Luzi, and the two gorgeous kids, all so nicely wrapped up!"

She kneels in front of the kids, who give her all their attention. Julia makes her excited cry, which she knows Sarah adores. Sarah uses both their names. After a short while, she gets up and shakes hands with Cassandra.

"Hello, I'm Sarah. You must be Cassandra; rumours spread. I'm Julia's sitter."

"Hello, yes. Glad to meet you, Sarah. Some rumours have reached the capital as well."

We all laugh and walk slowly along the pavement. Sarah talks mostly to me, I guess, but keeps her eyes on the kids.

"I expect it will look very different around here next spring."

I sense a question or a hope in her voice.

"Oh, yes indeed. Many people from a large area around Ore and even Hastings have offered us grown plants, flowers, bushes, even some small trees from their own gardens, so we wouldn't start all of it from seeds, small cuttings and sprouts. I guess we start mid too late March with our grass turf and slabs for the different paths around the garden. The rest will follow."

Cassandra looks surprised. "So, you'll have a full-grown lawn right away. Isn't that cheating?"

"Well, the first month, you must not step on the

grass and you must ensure the right amount of water. We will install an automatic sprinkler system at the same time. It draws water from our underground tank with rainwater collected from the surface of the house and garage. If frost goes into the soil, it may kill the small grass plants, but Julia is confident about it. It'll be OK, she says. It is an outside-time thing mixed with probabilities."

Sarah laughs. "So, typical Julia!"

It is interesting to see how the two small people walk side by side. I sense an inner dialogue between them, in pictures and super-brief video clips if I can say that, and general sensations connected to the visuals. I sense this without tapping into the content.

Julia connects to me while she still communicates with Walter.

"I know you wonder about Walter's life to come, and would like to share a glimpse of his bright future with Cassandra. That I will not give you. Walter has his own path, of course, but he has not come in to 'waste' it on mundane human experiences. He might join SAM and me in more than a consciousness connection, but I am not to talk about it and there is no reason for Cassandra to know anything about that. It will only shift her focus away from her primary task for the time being. A long time in human perspective."

EQ: Julia introduced SAM earlier in the series (Rider of the Crimson Dragon). He was the first to incarnate in a shell body, a body born initially without a soul, but only a connection to SAM. SAM embodied this body fully when it was about eight years old.

"That is clear talk. Thanks, Julia."

I sense a smile from Julia. "I know you only mean it in a good way, so Cassandra shouldn't worry about his future, but mums usually do. You know that, and, even so, you have a small degree of worry or maybe excitement about how my life as a fully embodied consciousness will be."

She gives me a hug as a sensual perception, and it is hard for me to hold back the tears.

Julia cries out. "Dad!"

She has spotted Ju-long and Karl coming towards us on the other side of the street. Ju-long crosses the street to prevent Julia from crossing. Not that many vehicles come here. She sets off, followed by Walter. Sarah is close behind to catch them if one should trip and fall.

Each father picks up their child and shortly after the children sit on their fathers' necks, where they bump up and down as they approach us. This is another common experience they can share.

Ju-long approaches us with a magnificent smile. "We found these two astronauts and want to invite them home for biscuits, rolls and cocoa."

I turn to Sarah. "Are you in for Ju-long and Julia's rolls and hot cocoa?"

"I know you wouldn't invite me if you didn't want to, so yes, I very much would like to."

Boomer shows up outside, just as we walk up to the front door at our house. Of course, she could hear us arriving from a distance. She uses her cat door in the laundry door to get in and receives us when we walk into the living room from the entrance hall.

Ju-long and Karl take over the kitchen, preparing the food, while us three girls takes care of the kids. Sarah sets the table. She knows where everything is.

When Julia and Walter return to the living room after getting fresh nappies, they continue their play at the low table next to the sofa. Sarah moves their plates from the dining table to the low table and replaces their personal two-handle cups with their feeding cups just as a precaution. She also serves rolls with butter on a plate to the two kids. When she returns to the dining table, she leans forward and whispers. "It will be interesting to see if they will share or fight over the rolls!"

Even though we do not bet, my wager is on the sharing, and I am right. Julia eats one half while Walter eats three. Later they come to get more to drink. They are adorable to watch. Boomer follows their play from her elevated post on the back rest of the sofa.

Later, after Sarah has left, four adults do their magic in the kitchen, while Walter and Julia do their artwork with extra thick bee's wax crayons. The crayons are handmade locally from bee's wax, organic pigments and other safe ingredients. I smile as I see Boomer asleep on the sofa on her back, showing her fluffy tummy.

After a not strictly Chinese New Year's dinner, Ju-long projects a short firework movie on the dome above our heads in the living room. After that, their dads put the kids to bed, while Cassandra and I finish up our wine and slowly clean up, making sure there is some work for the men when they return. Boomer has her meat in the kitchen and wanders outside in the dark to explore her realms of magic and wonders.

We enjoy a cosy evening, but I miss the fireplace from the house in Brighton. Ju-long and I had talked back and forth about a fireplace in the new house. We discarded the fireplace and are waiting to instal a wood burner later.

Sunday passes with much joy and laughter, and Cassandra and her family leave us shortly after lunch, taking the train back to London. It has been a wonderful weekend. Julia had especially enjoyed Walter's company. At one time the two were sitting side by side on the sofa with stretched legs, with Boomer lying across their legs and being stroked by the two. Boomer has grown large, and now she is so long that her legs hung down on the sofa at each side of the kids' legs.

What are thoughts?

Thoughts are the circular product of what the mind processes. In a quiet moment I turn to Saint Germain to get his wise words on the subject. I sense him before I can express my question.

"We have talked about the mind and the memory, but what are thoughts, really?"

Saint Germain does not appear in any describable form, and we do not meet in any realm. It is pure consciousness to consciousness, so I must "translate" our conversation.

"Thoughts happen in the limited human awareness, which then triggers the neurons and chemicals in the brain, which then again translates them into reality-projections on the human's event-screen. I call this event-screen B-O-N, but more details on the BON must wait for another time. The experience of reality is 'made' of your own energy; energy being communication, meaning there is no structure to this. There just SEEMS to be. Seeing an object goes like this: Object > Eyes > brain > sense of reality. It is YOUR eyes, YOUR brain and so YOUR interpretation of YOUR reality. Others can INFLU-ENCE the interpretation, but it is still YOU who interprets it with or through YOUR energy."

This logically leads to my next question. "How do I experience events with other people?"

"When you seemingly have the same experience as others, it is mostly the logical/mental or cognitive brain that interprets it in the same and limited way.

This is also because of the Atlantean linearization of the brain which again largely builds up the collective belief pool, mass consciousness."

We have moved away from the initial subject, even though this is quite interesting, so I bring us back on track. "Please, talk a little more about thoughts and memory."

"As I've said before, your memory, which is also information and judgements, is not in the brain. It is not even in the I Am. It is in your energy, in what I call your Devir, your energy pool. Here are also all future possibilities, not only on Earth but also what happens beyond that. It is not predetermined; there is no destiny here."

"What about the intelligence?"

"There is no intelligence in your energy. It appears when awareness and energy combine. There is no intelligence in the I Am either, but there is a knowingness, the Gnost. We have talked about the Gnost and we'll do it again some other time. The I Am doesn't make choices when it creates. That would limit it, and the I AM is unlimited."

"Can you talk a little more about the creation thing?"

"The I Am is the creator, but it is not creative. The I Am never uses intelligence in its creations, as stated before. It just creates. THEN it dives in and finds out what potentials it has created and the human then experiences those. The human turns the potentials into true/real creation, thus being the actual creator using the I Am's blueprint. The I Am radiates creations or possibilities, and the human aspect brings everything into experience by choice."

"I see that in creation there is no real intelligence as a person will know it. The so-called intelligence lies in which potential is picked."

"YES! Human or divine intelligence is not needed here. Therefore, there is none!"

I experience our communication constantly jumping off the subject, thoughts, and I realise it is all part of the same ... well, thing: the I Am experiencing its creations through the human.

Saint Germain had mentioned Atlantis was the primary cause for the collective belief pool. As I work on the question, I hear a doorbell ring.

"Strange! What's going on?"

Saint Germain smiles. "We have a visitor."

I sense a joyfulness joining us. "Here I Am, and I Am SAM!"

"Oh, hi SAM. It rhymes, Am and SAM. Are we in an excellent mood today?!"

"Today as always, and today is all we have!"

I sense Saint Germain laugh. "I'll leave you two to talk about Atlantis. Till next time, which is another today!"

SAM starts up right away. "In Atlantis we were communal and lived in and for the common society. That was why we worked hard to join our minds into a common or collective unit. We never realised we actually did it, because of our limited awareness. We also worked to embody our own essence, what we now call consciousness. This is the Atlantean Dream we pursue these days."

"Where did this all happen?"

"In the land of Alt, in the area called Atlan, there was the great city Tian, with its many temples. Here was the centre for research and teaching. You could say Tian is the centre of the Bermuda Triangle, which is more a circle. It is easy to see how the name of AtlanTian and Atlantis came to be. One of the other city names you find in this area is AtlanTa in the state of Georgia. Mexico City was the main city and one of the first established when people came to the Americas from Lemuria in the Pacific Ocean. Another city is today's Quito, the capital of Ecuador in South America."

"Why haven't we found anything from Atlantis, if a large part of it was in North America?"

"Archaeologists do not believe there was any occupation in that area until after the last Ice Age, so none of them have bothered looking. You can make a search for *The Younger Dryas Impact Hypotheses* on the Internet for more details. You will find that there were two major events and they had a huge impact on most of the planet."

I found that a cosmic impact suddenly melted a large amount of the ice cap, so meltwater, ice and mud levelled everything and covered the remains in mud. Meltwater that flowed into the oceans also temporarily stopped the Gulf Stream and a new Ice Age started.

"So an inland wave, not a sinking into the ocean, destroyed a large part of Atlantis. This part of Alt covered most of North America until the fall. The islands with the temples of Tian did eventually sink below the surface of the Atlantic Ocean due to the rise in sea level."

"Yes, Luzi. Landmasses can descend as well as rise into mountains quite fast, and the sea level will shift depending on how much of the water is bound as ice, primary at the planet's poles."

I have another question, now that I have SAM at first hand. "What are your and Julia's plans for working in the future?"

"We have no plans for the future, because, as I said, we only have today, but I know what you mean. Julia doesn't have to grow up before we can work together. We already do and have done for some time, dualistically speaking. I'll ask you to sense into what we do while I tell you that we work with consciousness dynamics by essentially break-ing down belief systems. This makes people less bounded to old ways and being controlled by old rules and more sensing into the truth of the mo-ment."

"It is actually working with New Energy!"

"It is. Cool, right?"

"How do you do the breaking-down thing?"

"As you do it, with your human connection, and other ways too. You've talked a lot about this subject, especially with Josela. Apart from working through the collective belief pool, we also work on the individual person's I Am to encourage people to recognise new ways of choosing instead of using old ways of that's-the-way-I've-always-done-it. Depending on the person, we can even encourage them to just allow New Energy to work and then see what comes out of it."

I surely remember my talks with Josela and the dragons, mostly as we meet in Elvendale.

"It's up to the person, then. If the person is open to communicate with the I Am, the human life turns out to be more joyful. More joyful, because of less resistance to change and therefore New Energy. I know it can be a slow and tedious process for the person to find the courage and trust at the moment that usually feels uncomfortable. Animals with low awareness will feel repelled by the area or even not realise it and will not enter."

After my communication with SAM, I feel uplifted by his joyful way. I also have a much deeper sense of connection and fulfilment, even though those words are inadequate.

Spring

I now shift the story to the early spring. It is Tuesday 3 March and Boomer's six-month birthday. In three days, Julia will be ten months old. Boomer has grown larger than a normal cat and has no problem defending her area around the house. Even the dominant male in the area knows his place. Boomer is more than a cat, so I guess that is the actual cause. Sekhmet had told me she and Boomer have made our plot a cat's heaven, a sanctuary where no aggressive acts are taking place. Even dogs can pass without causing trouble.

The weather is mild, with the right amount of rain, so we are not soaked in water that washes everything away. Ju-long and I work at home today, but right now we have taken a break and are working in the garden. Julia is in the nursery. We are removing the bark of the large tree branch with smaller branches we received from Gloria and Finn. This will be Boomer's tree in the living room and our decoration. We will shorten the branches and make a platform at the top for Boomer. Before getting the tree inside, Ju-long will burn the cleared surface with a blowtorch to make sure it is clean. The tree is too wide, so we must divide it into three sections to get it through the door, even though the door is wide. We will assembled it again with some large bolts.

This evening Boomer does not get special treats, but she and Julia share the bathtub which they both enjoy immensely. There is a lot of splashing and we get some good video shots to send to the family. Afterwards Julia helps her dad drying and brushing Boomer. The young cat enjoys it so much that she falls asleep in Ju-long's lap. He and Julia gently carry her to her box where she snuggles up with her bushy tail over her face.

Snow

Thursday, the day before Julia's nine-month birthday, we are in the kitchen in the afternoon making two layer cakes, one for the Artemis Nursery and one for ourselves. We will not be celebrating Julia's birthday, but, as she says: "We celebrate that we all connect on Earth at this special time in gratitude to our own magnificence."

Boomer looks at us from her new vantage post on the platform at the top of her tree in the living room, adding her essence as well.

The next day in the afternoon, as I arrive on my bike after picking Julia up at Artemis, she and I go inside to prepare tea for us, expecting Ju-long to arrive soon from Brighton. Julia's speech has greatly improved.

"We will make tea and cake for us and Dad."

As we walk into the laundry room, I notice Boomer on the floor meowing. If she spends time in here, she lies on the water pump to absorb the heat. With the direction of her sight, she moves my attention to behind Ju-long's rubber boots. Here I see a small white Maine Coon approximately the same size as Boomer when we got her. The kitten looks so adorable with her white fluffy fur and her big green eyes, and I am totally stunned. Julia squishes her way between my legs and the rubber boots.

"White Boomer!"

I move the boots, kneel and talk softly to the small kitten. Then I realise that she shouldn't be able to get through the cat door because we programmed it to only let Boomer pass. Boomer must have carried the kitten inside, holding it by the scruff of its neck, so her own neck was close enough to the cat door for her chip to activate it. Smart girl. Julia and I let the kitten sniff our hands, and then Julia gently touches her head. We manage to get the white kitten out into the middle of the floor, with Boomer and Julia in front of her. I hang up my coat and take Julia's as well, before I go to the locker where we keep Boomer's dry food, take a few and hand them to Julia. Now the kitten looks more curious than frightened as she sniffs the piece before eating it. This is a good sign. I turn to Boomer.

"Where did you find the kitten, dear?"

I get no response from either Boomer nor Sekhmet. It seems a little odd to me that Sekhmet does not respond. I turn to Julia.

"Let's take the kitten near Boomer's litter box. It's close to the dry food and the water fountain. Doesn't she look like a Snow White?"

Julia picks up the kitten, which seems content with

the handling. I now trust both Julia and Boomer concerning how they handle their lives. I open the door to the kitchen and we all head for the centre junction in the house. Julia puts down the kitten near the litter box, but the kitten seems fascinated by the fountain and walks close up to it.

"Julia, do you want to help with the tea and cake or stay with Boomer and the kitten?"

"Kitty will stay. I will help with the cake."

I am not so sure that the kitten will stay. It must come from somewhere and belong to someone. A Maine Coon represents a certain value to the owner, so I am sure she will be off sometime tomorrow.

Julia can set the low table by using her handcart to transport the things. Well, we drive the tea and the cake together.

I look at the cats from time to time. Boomer has taken the kitten to her box where they have snuggled up, while still keeping an eye on us.

We hear Ju-long closing the door to the room where we keep our bikes behind the garage and Julia runs to the laundry room to greet him. I can hear her excited voice. "White Boomer, white Boomer!"

"What is it with Boomer, dear?"

"Not Boomer, white Boomer!"

I poke my head into the laundry room and get a kiss.

"Boomer has brought a white Maine Coon kitten home."

Ju-long frowns while taking off his jacket. "Well, it can't be her own. She spends almost all her time here with us and there have been no signs of her being pregnant. We have to ask around."

"Yes, but first tea and layer cake. Julia has set the table!"

Julia takes her dad's hand. "First see kitten!"

Ju-long picks up Julia and follows where she points her index finger.

"Oh, she's so cute! Are we sure she's a female?"

I join the gathering. "No, actually not. If you can pick her up, we may find out."

Ju-long and I are sitting on the floor next to Boomer's box. After a few gentle strokes, Ju-long takes the kitten into his lap. He is able to turn her on her back so he can study the distance between the anus and the urinary tract opening. If the distance is short, relatively, it is a female. A larger distance indicates it is a male. We have photos of Boomer, so I run through the first ones and find a good one. We both agree, it is a male kitten.

"There goes my Snow White!"

Ju-long smiles. "How about White then?"

Julia climbs into her dad's lap where the kitten is

the right side up again.

"Snow, hi Snow!"

Ju-long chuckles. "Half of the name is better than none, right?"

I am a little worried on behalf of Julia, because we probably cannot keep the cat, and, if he already has a name, it might be something entirely different.

"Let's have some tea and cake. Julia, do you want tea too?"

She jumps down from Ju-long's lap. "Tea for me!" She takes my hand. "Snow can sleep with Boomer!"

The brazier has kept the tea warm so Ju-long mixes milk in Julia's tea to lower the temperature. She uses her two-handle cup, the step before using a normal cup with one handle.

After dinner and getting the girls and the boy in bed, Ju-long and I upload Snow's picture and description, and how and when we found him, or he found us, onto the different boards on the Internet. Tomorrow is Saturday, and we will post a paper on the board next to the way in to the village.

There was no response from owners on Saturday nor on Sunday, but we are sure that eventually we will be contacted by someone who claims the kitten. All responses were about how cute he looks.

It is Monday, and there have still been no claims on Snow. He has settled in fine and shares everything with Boomer. He gets half the portion of fresh meat that Boomer gets, and Ju-long has made a platform next to Boomer's at the top of the tree. We are both surprised he was able to climb the tree, but it didn't take him long to master it, even though the tree has no bark. The lower vertical stem has a coconut mat to hang on to, and the rest is soft enough to get the claws in. We heard a few bumps in the beginning when he fell to the floor, but when we checked he was OK.

Once again, I ask Sekhmet about Snow. This time she answers; not that I get more information.

"You are not supposed to know everything, my dear. He might tell you if, or when, he feels it is the right moment."

I had decided not to grow too attached to the kitten, but the white fur ball with the begging eyes enchants me again and again, so Snow gets at least as much attention from me as the rest of the family. On the weekend, when we usually talk to our family, both here in the UK and in Hong Kong, we get the same responses everywhere.

"Oh, wow, how cute. Such a lovely kitten!"

Anna even asks if she can have him.

Less than a minute after turning on the bed lamps this evening a soundless voice speaks to Ju-long and me.

"I appear to you as Seth, an aspect of me you might be slightly familiarly with."

I am the first to respond. "The Egyptian deity; not particularly popular, I believe."

I sense a smile. Friendly, not fierce. "Oh, the story, like most stories of old, is interpreted through the mind of now, even though people think they read the texts right. There was a different way of writing and reading millennia ago."

"So, you appear as Snow?"

"I could have appeared reddish or orange, like Boomer, for fire. In Egypt, I was the god of the red desert, but I chose white as the cleanser that clears things up."

Ju-long and I can feel an explanation coming as Seth continues." People are paradoxical in the sense that they want change from their misery, but, at the same time, they want things to stay the same, because that is what they know. Change may hurt because something must go, be destroyed, for change, or the new, to come in. In that sense, Seth is a purifier who breaks down the old to make way for the new."

A little like the black dragon, Knight, that rearranges and collects aspects, bringing things into harmony. So, what one could see as the darkness could be seen as a bringer of harmony. Likewise, the destroyer that brings in clarity and space for renewal.

Seth smiles again. "There are always two sides on a

coin in duality. It is just a matter of which side you look at."

I return the smile. I even have a smile on my face in the dark bedroom. "Simply put, Seth breaks habits."

"In a sense, I energetically ask people if they are ready for change. If they respond in their energy, I give them permission to do so. I don't want to do it for them, nor can I."

Ju-long, being practical, asks the consciousness that appears as Seth, "So, I can assume that no one will show up to claim Snow?"

"Oh no, Snow is his very own."

My smile broadens. "Another multi-layered member in the family, then!"

"Yes, we are just about to be called a crowd."

Ju-long dares another question. "Many things must change around here. You come in to assist these changes to take place."

"Indeed, young man, indeed. Sekhmet and I work together very well. And remember, we are multi-tools. Focusing on only one thing seems a little limited, don't you think?"

Snow gets his vaccinations and a chip to control the cat door. The vaccinations are to please the system, of course. We set his birthday to 6 January 2020, two months before he showed up, which was also Julia's eight-month birthday.

The different work groups in the village had meetings around 1 March to fine-tune the plans for the early spring and get more content on the plans for the rest of the year if possible.

The families who use rainwater to flush the toilets must use filters and UV-light to kill microorganisms or they will thrive in the toilet and leave discolorations. These are not prevalent in the winter, but when things come to life in spring, it will be a real challenge. It is still not perfect, and they must find a solution or simply give up using the gathered rainwater for toilet flushing. I come up with the idea of adding salt, though it is not perfect because it can corrode the pipes if they are not of plastic or stainless steel; or the salt may crystallise if the solution is too strong. Someone suggests large sediment filters.

We have a water tank collecting rainwater from the dome house, but it will only be used for watering the garden. We use particle filters to prevent objects from getting stuck in the sprinkler system. These filters have a back-flush system, which uses some of the already filtered water pumped backwards into the filters to clean them to some degree. A barrow with a tap collects this small amount of water so it's used to water manually. If not used here, it is led into the drain.

This weekend we shape the earthwork around the house so it is ready to receive first the stone slabs for the garden paths and later the lawn turf, plants, bushes and small trees. A landscape architect living in the village instructs us and others during this weekend, so the entire area looks like an ant hill during the daylight hours. Margaret has an exceptionally good imagination and sees how the garden will look when it is in full bloom. She is one of the people who made and maintains the 3D-map programs and materials of all houses and the whole topography of the village, including roads and the layout of pipes and electrical wires.

Next weekend is garden-path weekend. Most families will dig out for the pavement, add sand and lay slabs and gravel. During the next week, all materials will arrive for the entire village. This is also the time when our lawn turf will arrive from southern France. We plan to lay it out on the weekend after the garden paths are in place. Most families will sow the grass, but we want the garden to be ready as fast as possible for Julia and now the two cats. Dad, and possibly also Mum, will show up to lend a helping hand with installing the automatic sprinklers and add the program to the house's management system on its special computer in the laundry room. The guide cables for the two lawnmower robots will also be laid into the ground.

Knight in the moonlight

The black dragon Knight shows up Sunday night when I wake up just past midnight.

"I am here to invite you on a walk through a landscape at night."

"Indeed, you lead the way."

We are pure consciousness with no shapes when we appear in a rocky terrain with some vegetation. The air is still kept warm by the surroundings, beaming the warmth collected from the sun. There are low cliffs on both sides of a narrow path cleared of rubble, which we follow. It feels as though we glide side by side, even though we have no bodies. The moon is almost full and shines a dim light over the landscape. The rocks and boulders create shadows which could be cave entrances or just surfaces in the dark. I am not afraid and feel totally safe. We glide a while in silence so I can adjust to the scenery. Eventually, Knight breaks the silence, but without speaking out loud.

"This walk is to show your scattered and hiding parts, that you, the Master, are truly ready to receive them home into your essence. It will show them that you are not a weak fairy, but one who can stand her ground and bring all back into unity."

"I know they need to see me as strong and powerful, even if those concepts no longer are a part of what defines me. If I appear as weak, as they feel they are themselves, they will despise me and can't use me as the captain of the ship, or may even challenge me for the position."

"You are correct, Luzi. We use the moonlight to lure those out who are ready to join the whole. If they have the courage to move into the moonlight, which is actually your light, they are ready."

"I see. If they are too scared or repulsed by my appearance, they won't come out."

"You are right again, dear. There will come another one who will deal with the last clearing. More precisely, I should say another part of you. I am the nurturer and keeper of the discarded ones. Your 'house' will be cleared out little by little."

As we move up the path, I sense entities or pieces of consciousness with very various amounts of self-awareness. They represent all kinds of lower emotions from deep sorrow to wild rage and complete madness.

"I can sense them. It's not pleasant, but I know it's all me, or part of what I as different entities, not always as a human, have created."

Knight is very present, but not protective, since I need no protection.

"You are here to show yourself and ALLOW the homecoming, not to communicate or invite anyone home. It must be their own choice or it won't work."

"Yes, I understand that. But there are SO many and

I understand why. Each human persona can produce myriads of dark entities during one lifetime, so it sums up."

No entity shows up or joins us during our long parade. I sense it is their decision, their CHOICE to come home, which is of importance here.

The path curves to the right and grows steeper. It stops at the top of a flat cliff where we can overlook the path we have already travelled. I sense the trip ends here. In a hollow in the flat cliff there is a small pond where the moon above us is reflected. As I stare at the circle, I end up staring at the ceiling in our bedroom, sensing Ju-long sleeping next to me. I thank Knight for the walk, and he greets me before he withdraws his focus.

The black soil of Meso-America

Our plants group in the village has been looking into the remarkable *terra preta*, Amazonas' black soil that has a high concentration of carbon. It was formed 2500 years ago by the native Americans.

Here are some of the contents: Charcoal, prepared with low temperatures so it attracts nutrients. There are ashes, plant material and compost, animal manure, human excrement, crushed pottery and pot shards. It also contains bones, tortoise shells, egg shells, mineral-rich dirt which could be from quarries or river sediments from the mountains. There is also a large microbial diversity, including predominantly fungal.

Seen from a chemist's viewpoint: phosphorus, nitrogen, calcium, magnesium and especially carbon. The pH is, ranging from 5.2 to 6.4, which is good for retaining moisture.

The charcoal seems to be important, so we should char plant materials rather than compost them, but with low temperature. Plant material also contains microorganisms, so not all should be charred.

Before our meetings, I didn't know there was any difference between organic, ecological, and biodynamic farming.

Organic farming: no use of pesticides, artificial fertiliser, genetically modified seeds.

Ecological farming adds the following to the list: minimisation of waste production and recycling the waste. There is also a focus on vegetation around the crops that increases the welfare of the fauna like bees and other pollinators and woodland birds.

Biodynamic farming is much like organic farming, with an esoteric overlay derived from Dr Rudolf Steiner.

Where do farm animals fit into all this? Organic farming also talks about antibiotics, growth hormones and general animal welfare. While meat contains less antibiotic resistant bacteria, I wonder how high the ethics is to make sure animals get treated with antibiotics if NEEDED to get well. The animals must be fed organically, and with food as close to their natural diet as possible.

The groups connecting to farming and, to some degree, gardening have their focus on anything from the surrounding fauna and flora to fish farming, shellfish and seaweed, to eco-friendly washing powder and what food restaurants serve. People are very passionate about their different subjects, and talks and sometimes loud discussions may go on for hours.

Mum and Dad visit

There has been a slight change in plans after talking to my parents this weekend. At the dinner table, before we call my parents, Julia turns to me and says, loud and clear, "Ya and Carl are coming soon!"

"Yes, in two weeks. The weekend after this one."

"No, soon!"

Then she turns her attention to her food. Ju-long and I look at each other, and I shrug my shoulders.

Our plan was for Mum and Dad to help install the sprinklers and the lawnmower robots the week after next, when we have laid the slabs around the garden, the entrances and the garage.

After dinner we call up Ya and Carl on the computer for a videoconference. Julia rarely says Grandma and Granddad. I guess it is more natural to use their names, because her DNA is shifting from what she inherited from Ju-long and I to her very own and unique blueprint.

When we talk, Dad suggests that we place the sprinkler hoses, the moisture sensors and the wire guides for the robots at the same time as the slabs, so all will be ready for us to roll out the lawn turf the weekend after. Now we all look forward to Mum and Dad visiting us next weekend. Ju-long must have all the materials ready a week before our original plan. Slabs, sand and machinery have been taken care of, so it will be wires, electrical valves for the water, fittings, humidity sensors, sprinkler heads and a lot of water hose. I guess we will make a family trip to the DIY (do it yourself) centre Monday or Tuesday for the common things. The rest Julong has already ordered.

We have agreed that Mum and Dad should not bring any playground things before we can walk on the grass. I know that my sister, Anna, wants to be part of building a sandbox and other things. She has her own things to tend to in London and elsewhere, so we see little of her down here in Hastings. I can't keep track of her exams at the university. That is more a job for Mum.

Mum and Dad arrive early Friday afternoon from their home in Sevenoaks. They bring lovely raw ingredients and want to make dinner. Jo-long has a workday at home, and he has picked up Julia early from the nursery so they can do some baking together.

I have had a working day at the University of Kent at the Tonbridge Centre and arrive at Hastings at the Ore station at 4:30 p.m. When using the train between Hastings and Tonbridge, I can enjoy passing through the vast farmland and forests all the way, and it is more relaxing than driving myself.

As I walk in through the front door, I have a young girl and two eager cats around my legs greeting me. Julia wants to show me a four-legged easel given to her by her grandparents, for the most part Mum, I guess. We can use it both on the floor and on a table. Very practical. Julia has already made the first artworks.

By the smell of food in the house, I figure my parents have taken over the kitchen.

"Welcome, dear!" Mum shouts from the open kitchen area while Dad approaches me wearing Julong's flowery apron.

"Hello, dear!"

He hugs me without touching me with his hands. I bet he has his hands full with something wonderful in the kitchen.

He looks down at the cats and Julia. "The girls have grown since I saw them last time, and Snow is even more charming than on the videos. The family is growing!"

I remember Julia's remark about a brother, but I shut it out. I have my hands full with family, work, house and garden for the moment.

Julia appears in my thoughts, painting a scene.

"But in autumn, when you've installed a wood burner, with the rain and the storm outside and only candles burning in the living room, it will be so romantic!"

At first I feel a little angry towards her for mingling in my life, but then I sense the wonderful love from this great being and I send a warm hug back.

"I know he waits to join us, your brother!"

I kiss the small ones, then Mum and Ju-long. Julia takes my hand and leads me to the low table by the sofa to show me a painting she has made with water colours.

At first it just looks like two blobs, a black over a blue, but then she explains to me and the picture becomes clear. "Granny in China!"

Now I see a walking lady, almost from the back, in a traditional, expensive Asian dress and her hair gathered on top of her head. She only lacks an umbrella to make the picture perfect. There is no head and neck, though.

"Oh, indeed. It is great-grandma Jiang in Hong Kong!"

I take a photo of the painting on the easel and the artist next to it. The two cats in the tree show up in the background.

I call out to the others. "Have you all seen this?"

Julia talks to me without words. "The brain is pretty good at adding the dots, so to speak, bringing meaning to two blobs, as you call them. I rarely bring up this kind of family information, but you might all want to take a trip to Hong Kong in late autumn."

I understand. My grandma, the last of my grandparents, is seventy-six this autumn, and her husband passed over a few years ago. Her name, Jiang, means river, so I guess she will soon find a new direction to steer her flow.

They can all see the lady now. I catch Mum's eyes. "Maybe we should visit her this autumn? It will be the first time Julia has visited Hong Kong."

I see Dad gets the message too. "What a splendid idea. Good thinking, Julia."

Dad is more intuitive than one would think, and he has a strong connection to Julia. He knows it was not my idea.

At dinner, Julia gets a lot of attention from her grandparents. Understandable, because she is very charming and holds her focus on the two. She uses short sentences and mind pictures, and it works very well. I have placed my parents on the same side of the table, with Julia at the head, so she needs only to turn her head to one side to communicate. Ju-long and I sit opposite my parents. The cats get their raw meat in the kitchen.

The food is delicious, and Dad has brought home-made ice cream for dessert. We are all pretty full afterwards.

Later, after Julia has been tucked in, the two cats enjoy a grooming session with Mum and Dad. It seems the two humans enjoys it as much as the cats, which are completely apathetic afterwards and are tucked in as well. Now we can do a little planning for tomorrow's work. I have a large print-out of the garden from Elisabeth, the garden architect. Dad does most of the drawing of where to place the sprinklers and the humidity sensors. The wires will be put into white plastic tubes so they are protected, and also easy to spot if someone digs a hole later. We arrange that Mum is mostly with Julia, but since we have almost two days, there will be time for walks and the like where we are all together.

When we are in bed, Ju-long tells about his experience when we talked about my grandma earlier.

"When you were talking about visiting Hong Kong, I got a picture of my grandparents as we met them after they had died."

"Indeed, it will be another goodbye. The last one to that generation."

"Does Jiang know herself?"

We sense Julia nodding. I turn my focus to Grandma and I sense her rejoicing. Human death is always a great relief, even if most people fear the moment. If one is aware, it is a great relief when one can shed the physical body.

The next day, Saturday, is our busiest day. We work on getting water hoses and wires in the ground and place sprinklers and sensors right using measuring tapes. We dig out so we can lay the slabs in sand. Ju-long and Dad do the job with the slabs of natural stone. We mark everything on the large drawing and even take photos. The guide wires that mark the parameters for the two lawnmowers are the most critical to place at the right depth. They must be in the ground to prevent damage from the activities on the surface, but not too far down, or the robots will have trouble sensing them. The robots will also have an internal map with areas off-limit. It will make it easier for them to plan their route and to navigate. Elisabeth will update the ground plan on the computer later.

In the afternoon, we take time to walk around the village to see how the rest of the families are doing.

As we pass Jacob and his family's plot, I see Sarah is getting dirty in her working clothes, but she seems to enjoy what she is doing. The family comes over to the pavement for a brief talk. Jacob tries to be funny.

"I see you're already planting stuff, but I'm not sure they will grow no matter how much you water them!"

"Jar, Jar," Julia greets him. She can say Jacob now, but the name seems to stick on the large friendly man, and I am sure he doesn't want it to be any different. I always think about the *Star Wars* character Jar Jar Binks; because of the name, not the appearance.

We have Julia's pushchair with us, but she prefers to walk. Jacob bends down to greet her.

"Dear princess, you look so lovely today. And you have Grandma and Grandpa visiting. That is great!"

Julia spreads her arms and Jacob lifts her up.

"Higher!"

Jacob places her on his broad shoulder and she laughs out loud. She knows the big man adores her.

"You will soon have a pleasant garden to play in. That'll be great!"

"Boomer and Snow will play too!"

"Yes, they will, and they'll have some trees to climb too. I'm impressed how good you speak at such a young age."

"Thanks, you too!"

I can see that Jacob had not expected such a comment. Julia sends me a brief message, and I explain to the man.

"She wants to be polite and what she means is that you are good in choosing the right words. You didn't say: 'how fast you have learned to speak'. You focused on the quality. Her physical body just needed to mature to use speech."

Jacob smiles.

"Now I'll put you down again so you don't get sick of being so high up."

As he puts her on the ground, she looks into his eyes, shaking her head, and smiles. Then he brings forth a roaring laughter.

"She said as clear as if it came from her mouth that I must be careful myself, because I have my head that high up most of the time."

We all part with a smile. Dad is proud of his granddaughter. "Only ten months old and already able to fend for herself in an argument with a grown man!"

Julia takes his hand and we continue our walk. When we come back, Julia and Mum prepare the afternoon tea. The cats are out, so Julia takes an afternoon nap alone after the tea.

We work as long as we have sunlight, and when we get in around 6 p.m., we are pretty tired, but in a good way. A lovely smell of food greets us as we walk into the kitchen from the laundry room. The cats are back too, waiting for their meat. Julia is up from her nap and has been driving everything in her handcart to the dining table. Mum just had to put it on the table.

When it is time for Julia to go to bed, Dad tucks her in. He reads Richard Bach's *There's No Such Place As Far Away* for her. (See Addendum in the back of the book for details).

When Dad is back, we give a status report on our progress and what we still need to do. Everything regarding the sprinkler system is in place. The water hoses had to be dug in the deepest. Everything that goes under the slabs is in place as well. First, we had planned digging the rectangular hole for Ju-long's halfdown-dug greenhouse, so we didn't have to bring in a big digger over the slabs and playground later. Now we see we can bring a small digger in via the path to the right of the house. The greenhouse will be next to the compost to draw carbon dioxide from the rotting plants, which is then used to feed the greenhouse plants. The playground has been prepared by removing part of the top soil so we can fill the shallow hole with bonded-rubber eco-mulch. Rubber shreds, bonded with a high-performance polyurethane resin, are installed to create a seamless playground surface with no loose particles. It appears similar to a bark or wood-chip surface; the key difference is that it is bound and does not erode or deteriorate. We can lay it out in different colours and patterns. Mostly what we need to do tomorrow is the runway to the garage and the rooms behind it, the extra parking space next to it, and to brush more sand between the slabs already laid in the garden.

The next morning Dad is up early, at about seven, making pancakes and other lovely stuff. Julia comes into our bedroom with a piece of pancake made from spelt in her hand. Ju-long lifts her up in the bed. She wants us to taste it, so we do. I can smell new-brewed coffee, so I put on my dressing gown and walk to the bathroom. Our Sunday has started.

Even though our two cats are embodied by consciousnesses or higher beings using them for a firm connection to Earth, we in the family usually see them as our pets and treat them as such. After being in the bathroom, I say good morning to Dad in the kitchen. Mum is in the other bathroom. On my way to get dressed, I see the two cats sitting in the tree in the living room watching Dad with keen interest, waiting for him to serve their raw meat.

I meet Julia who is on her way out of our bedroom. She asks where she can find her grandma.

"Oh, I just heard her in the small bathroom. She'll come out soon. While you wait, please ask Granddad to find food for Boomer and Snow. You can feed them in their bowls."

Only wearing her nappy, she walks to the kitchen. I love her so much, that little thing!

Before breakfast I breastfeed her and then she sits in her high chair, sharing what we get. Her favourites are finger food of fruit and vegetables, and also juice. She has told us that getting juice into her mouth, especially from fruit, feels like an explosion of taste, so we add water to her juice. Here I can mention that all her four molars have broken through the gums, which has increased her appetite for solid foods. She is not too fond of porridge, but she prefers porridge from maize and sometimes from rolled oats. She doesn't want cow's milk.

After breakfast, Grandma gives Julia a bath in the bathtub, and they have a great time. No cats are allowed in the bathtub this time, so they come out to the rest of us in what will become the garden. After having explored a bit, they leave us to the northwest for a small gathering of trees and, a little further, the Bourne Stream.

Under the slabs leading from the sidewalk to the front and back door and the slabs in front of the garage and the extra parking space next to it, we laid a plastic tube in spirals. This tube connects to some heat pipe loops drilled 240 feet or 80 meters vertically into the ground. This system is filled with anti-frost liquid. A solar-powered pump circulates the liquid that brings warmth from deep down, keeping the slabs dry and free from snow and ice in the winter. The pipes are drilled vertically so they don't conflict with the horizontal air pipes also in the ground, which bring warm air to the house in cold times and cool the house in warm times. Well, the air temperature from the pipes is the same, but used for different purposes depending on the temperature in the house.

The work takes longer than I expected, so it is good that Dad got us started early. We are quite tired when we finish up for a late dinner in the evening. I had expected my parents to leave in the late afternoon, but now they stay another night. Julia, Ju-long and I are happy to have them, so that is fine. Julia wants them to drive her to the nursery Monday morning. Ju-long will leave for Brighton, but I will work at home.

Ju-long and I will spend the next weekend in the garden. The rolls of lawn turf have arrived, just waiting to paint a large part of the black soil in our garden green.

There is a lot of work going on in the village during the next week; especially, hedges are being planted. I also see some fruit trees and berry bushes in the black soil.

Most of the slab-paved paths in the garden are wide enough for a small garden tractor to pass. This makes it easier to bring the rolls of grass to where we will roll them out. We are quick to get the hang of it, and the work is in good progress. It still takes us two days to finish the work, because we have to take care of Julia most of the time even though Sarah visits us for a few hours in the afternoon. She works at her parents' garden as well, and she also has her college work to do.

It would have been an advantage to put plants, bushes and trees into the soil before rolling out the lawn turf, but it is still early for some vegetation because the handling would stress them. On the other hand, hedges, bushes and trees that drop their leaves are at rest in the cold period, so this would be the best time to plant those. We can plant evergreens all year. The general challenge all families face is that the soil around their houses has been a building site until November or December last year. The earthwork must be arranged and have time to settle before a garden can be established with success.

Two weeks later, Monday 6 April, it is Julia's eleven-month birthday. We are talking with our families on Hong Kong Island. In the morning, our time, we talk with Julia's great grandma Jiang at the retirement home. She sits in the home's computer room, where they do all kinds of fancy work and also make video calls to friends and family. She has an early afternoon tea. She looks and sounds fine, but is as old as I remember her. I come to think of our autumn visit to Hong Kong, which will be our last farewell in the physical world.

After Grandma, we talk with Ju-long's biological dad, Kong, whom I have come to appreciate very much. I think of how he opened to us a couple of years back and I get tears in my eyes. I stand behind Ju-long who stands behind Julia, sitting in her high chair in front of the computer. Kong seems to thrive and deeply appreciates life.

When Julia returns from the nursery in the afternoon, we call up Ju-long's mother, Ting, and her husband, Cheng. It is just before they go to bed. They always work long hours, but enjoy the creation involved. They are both gentle people. We talk about their upcoming visit to England, staying here for Julia's one-year birthday on 6 May 2020. Dad has made the travel arrangements, and I know they will use business class. I remember Dad saying, "I don't want to see two exhausted Chinese getting out of the plane when I pick them up at Heathrow!"

Cheng tells us it will be a twelve-hour non-stop flight. I know he has done this many times before, as part of his business as a salesman for his Chinese food products all over the world, but I guess mostly in Europe. He will NOT be in a crammed seat for twelve hours, and I totally agree with him.

A long-awaited visit

Late spring

Monday 20 April; the lawn should be stable enough to walk on. The status is: it is. FINALLY! We have had no frost on the ground since we laid the lawn, otherwise we would have laid out reed mats to protect the tender plants. I had been worried if too much rain came that it would drown the roots, because they need air around them too, but the grass looks healthy and the ground feels steady to walk upon. It had helped me enormously getting messages from the caretakers out there. We have "little folk" different from the ones in Brighton, but those here are well capable of their jobs. Julia has told us she has observed them being quite interested in the new installations in the village. Ju-long and I look forward to being more engaged in their work so we can learn from them and join for a common good. Writing this, I remember Ju-long's mum, Ting, had visited us a couple of years back. She and I had been in the garden in Brighton enjoying all life there, including the white dragon, Loong, though invisible. We shed a lot of tears that day.

Talking about Ting, she and Cheng will arrive at Heathrow the Monday before Julia's first-year birthday on Wednesday 6 May. Dad will not drive from Sevenoaks to Heathrow to pick them up at 3:30 a.m. He will stay in London and pick them up from there. We Hong Kongers know that sleeping the last hours before landing, especially at the midnight take off, might help us back in shape one or two days earlier than it may take otherwise.

We spend a lot of time in the garden these days, enjoying the greenness between the winding paths. Ju-long tests the two lawnmower robots, and Julia and the cats are very fascinated by them. They are used to VW, the two cleaner robots in the house, so they are not afraid of the lawnmowers. The two green robots come out from their low house like two spiders—well, SLOW spiders—and the cats are immediately on top of one of them. Julia is way overexcited and cries out in joy. New playmates, I guess. Ju-long laughs.

"We could call them T1 and T2 for turtle one and two instead of just #1 and #2 like Carl has named them."

"Whatever makes you happy, dear!"

I guess they had just gone from slow spiders to fast turtles. Not bad. I hope they don't eat everything in Ju-long's vegetable garden later this year.

You may ask about the playground, but it is here where Julia's birthday comes in, including Anna's self-built sandbox. Not that we will put everything up at once, but when it is done, the bonded-rubber eco-mulch will finish the colourful sculptures. I have asked Julia how she would react to a playground, well knowing that she is not a small child in her consciousness, and I was surprised by her answer.

"In a sense, the I Am IS like a child in total surprise and joy of its creations. It never stops. Just remember your sister when you visited Ocean Park in Hong Kong last time. She was twenty-four and said that, while it was not the same as when she was a young kid, she still enjoyed shooting the water cannons at people. She even admitted that."

"Yeah, but a see-saw, swings or a short slide?"

"Don't see it from a grown-up's perspective. If you do, everything seems dull. You must see it through the eyes of a child; that's the whole point of it. Adults attending a child on the playground will, to some extent, relive their own pleasureful moments when they were children. I have had many childhoods, and many were less joyful than could have been seen with human eyes, so I know how to cherish those blessed moments."

Plants have come in from people mostly in and around Hastings. Donations you could call them. People would have composted the plants otherwise. Now we have some full-grown or good starter plants to give new homes.

Our three kids are pretty dirty when we get inside, so Ju-long and I give them a thorough bath in the bathtub, only wearing underwear ourselves. It is fun as always, but it bites us back, because there is a lot of hair and fur to deal with right after the bath. On the other hand, during the grooming the kids get very drowsy and take a nap in the Boombox afterwards. Now the adults have a little time for themselves.

At the beaches of Elvendale

This morning, I wake up at 4:56 a.m. with a question for Saint Germain. I have never been to the seashores of Elvendale and want to see it, so I ask Saint Germain to meet me there. As we meet, he is in a pleasant mood; which he usually is, I must add.

"You don't have to come up with a question to meet your favourite count."

He pauses briefly and gives me a hug. Then he points to the eastern horizon. "I chose an early sunrise for the scenery. When you wake up in your bed, you are soon to be up anyway."

"Oh, hello, my favourite count! What lovely scenery. I actually HAVE a question for Your Grace."

The seashore lies beyond Elvendale City, the Great Lake and some low mountains. I can see the tallest part of the city through a crack in the mountains, and I can see the mountains inland as well. It is still very early, but the sun shows us where it will come over the horizon to our right. It has given the low clouds their first faint colours.

Conveniently, there is a nice bench facing east towards the sunrise, which is forty-five degrees off from the horizon over the sea, where a bench would usually point. Saint Germain's comment is there immediately. "Why turn your head, when you can turn the bench?"

I pose my question. "As it is now, the default backdrop for a person's life is mass consciousness and ancestral 'karma'. Sad to say, in a way. My question is, dear count: Who or, better, what creates a typical human's life?"

"The I Am is simply rejoicing the 'I Exist' in awareness. It has no memory of anything. The I Am is radiant. You may say that the human is at the end of a ray, experiencing life. The I Am does NOT create your human reality."

As we dive into the beautiful play in ever-changing colours and non-earthly music, I respond to the comment. "It should be obvious that the I Am doesn't create the human reality and then let the human, like a puppet on a string, play in that reality. It would really be how a human might think a god would act. This must be the true meaning of free will."

"The human, as an aspect of the I Am, chooses the possibility, the reality, through its choices and belief systems and the perception of it. The I Am is still just awareness. The human dives into this creation and experiences and expresses itself through its own perception and awareness. Ideally, this should be done in the same joy as the I Am experiences itself in its I Exist, but, as you know, this is seldom the case."

Everyone who believes life must be hard accepts conditions that are not true. I don't blame anyone and can, to an extent, see how this comes to be.

"So, the human got lost in itself and its creations. I see it here as the mind with its thoughts and emotions causing this."

"True creation is, as you know, without agenda, with no expectation of a specific outcome, or any outcome for that matter, but as the human mind, well, gets a mind of its own, conditions come in."

"So, you're particularly witty today, sir!"

"Aren't I always?!"

We laugh, and then Saint Germain continues. "True creation is like the I Am saying, 'I create' and then diving into one of the possibilities in the creation, in this case the human life."

I get a video clip for my inner eyes of the I Am as a person who jumps into the pool while the pool and the water is still being created and hits the surface just as the water forms and the pool comes into existence.

"So, where is the I Am in relation to the human?"

"Allow the Master Wisdom to guide you up and down the ray of creation I told you about before, to let you be in the perception of the awareness of the I Am together with the Master Wisdom. At the same time, you know that there is no ray of energy and no master entity."

I imagine myself slowly moving up and down a yellow beam of fairy dust together with an undefined figure, and Saint Germain comments. "This experience is distilled into wisdom instantly, so the energy here is Living Energy, because there are no layers of old unprocessed experiences. You own the energy; it is yours."

"Living Energy?"

"Old energy was responsive and suits duality; new energy is a dynamic and living energy, interacting with the Gnost. Here you are in the Gnost, not in your mind. Gnost is the guiding system when the mind is truly in total rest in the human life. At some point, we'll talk more about the Gnost."

Now the sun brings an explosion of kaleidoscopic colours to the land of Elvendale and the music around us rises to new heights. I look inland and suck up the whole scenery to keep and cherish it for eternity. I give the dear count a hug and turn my focus away from Elvendale.

Back and conscious in my body next to Ju-long, I can clearly see why peoples' lives are in such a mess. By mess, I simply mean that their lives are truly not what they really want them to be. They can't be, because what creates their lives is not theirs for the most part. It is mass consciousness and their ancestors! I actually know that, but this is just so CRAZY. A person doesn't run its own program on her or his computer, but ANYONE else's, like in the millions! No wonder things get stuck.

As I have talked about before, each person must clear attachments to mass consciousness and ancestors and allow its lingering aspects home. This will create a platform or base to interact with the world in a truly personal way.

I remember a picture of the Egyptian pharaoh Akhenaten standing under a sun disk which casts many beams, all with hands at the end. Then it hit me: he was not talking about ONE GOD, but the I Am connecting to many lives of its creation. Akhenaten might not have fully understood the concept he was given, but the biblical Moses could have brought the teachings out of Egypt. The sun disk, the rays, the hands, equals The Father which equals The I Am. The Holy Spirit is the creator energy, and the Son the human. When the mind can't grasp the simplicity and at the same time the grandness of this, namely being god also, but not the biblical one, then the explanation it comes up with must be of the human world.

Pharaoh Akhenaten (right) and queen Nefertiti.

As a detail in the relief, you can see a beam with an Ankh symbol reaching down to Akhenaten and Nefertiti. The Ankh is said to symbolise life, but I will be more specific and call it consciousness or the Master Wisdom connecting them to the I Am. If it just meant life, it would not have been used the way it was in old pictures and writing.

I can see they use the SAME sun (the I Am), but this is how Akhenaten saw the concept. The Egyptians should worship him and his queen, and he should have the connection to the sun. This reminds me of priests being mediators between man and god. Separation gives power to the mediators, whether they are aware of it or not.

While we look forward to the visit from Hong Kong and being with Ting, Cheng, Mum, Dad and Anna again, the garden looks nothing like it did in the winter, all bare and muddy. Now there is vegetation everywhere, except most of Ju-long's vegetable garden. The construction of the compost section and Ju-long's greenhouse is almost finished, and he hopes to close the greenhouse and make the carbon dioxide intake together with the ventilation and the water system ready before Julia's birthday. It is all run from the computer in the laundry room, which also controls the rest of the automated systems.

Cheng has a few selected customers he sees as friends whom he will visit together with Ting while they are in Europe. One of them lives in Brighton, the very place where he and Ting first met. They will go to London too.

Ju-long and Julia have full British citizenship, and we all have dual citizenship, like Anna, Mum and Dad, so we are also Hong Kong citizens or Hong Kongers. I will enjoy the spring and summer and not get emotional about why we are taking the trip to Hong Kong in the autumn.

The headbands in Atlantis

From time to time I sense a blockage, like having a metal helmet over my head or mind, as if my awareness is locked in, not being able to soar freely. I form this as a question, and Knight the black dragon comes into my awareness, inviting me to Elvendale. I end up at the rim of the mighty volcano to the north-west of Elvendale City and wonder why Knight has chosen to answer that question and why he has picked the volcano as the place for the meeting.

I feel the compassion of the magnificent dragon, compassion that you might call love, but it is so much more. I sense Knight being gentle, maybe even joyful as I look into his beautiful crystal-blue eyes.

"You are in a good mood today, Knight."

"Indeed, we will cover a large part of what I have been carrying around for the human you in all your lifetimes."

"Oh, it's good to address things so they can be cleared out and integrated. What is the subject that will cover the blockage I encounter?"

"We'll be talking about guilt. Especially guilt from your lives in Atlantis. Guilt is a huge part of what is tucked away in the darkness, but first something about Atlantis; something you already know, but you haven't quite realised how large a part of it you were or how directly involved you were."

I sit down, leaning my back up against Knight's neck as he rests on the red soil that covers the top of the rim. I both hear and feel his breath and heartbeat while he continues telling about Atlantis.

"With the intention of making everyone ONE, to experience every event in life alike, they manipulated the minds with energy by influencing the brain with headbands. This didn't really bring oneness, but total separation, limitation AND uniformity, which could be seen as oneness because all was alike."

"So, the headbands are what I sense now and then."

"You and many others were directly responsible for this and have accumulated an enormous guilt because of it. It was not intentional, but this way the I Am experienced total separation from itself. It is the headbands you sense AND their strong connection to the guilt surrounding them. The guilt— well, any guilt—is not valid, because there is no right or wrong here, just experience and wisdom."

"How did the headbands work?"

"The headbands were a combination of crystals and metal, and tuned so when you wore one of them and entered one of the chambers, a very loud banging noise or energy was pumped into the mind one pulse about every two seconds. The next generations and others inherited the alterations through mass consciousness. All became trapped in the mind; you were held in the mind. Now it's time for you to set yourself free of the mind and its limitations."

"Did everyone take those treatments?"

"Only the upper classes wore them. It was a sign of status to be allowed the headband treatments. Some of you, who could have worn the headbands, chose not to wear them. They were still influenced during other lives through mass consciousness."

"So, you are here to help me with this."

"The human can't fix this total separation nor the guilt. The final clean-up must come from the I Am. The energy must be released again. You can allow it, that's all. Releasing this will ultimately bring the potential for others to do the same."

"Like Saint Germain said to me, it's all about allowing. After going through this, the experience will go into mass consciousness and be a potential for others to pick up when they are ready."

From the edge of the volcano, I look into the deep crater where a little smoke rises from the black depths of which I can't see the bottom.

"Why are we here at the top of this volcano, Knight?"

"The volcano is the furnace that purifies everything in Elvendale. Just as Loong has told you some time ago. It also symbolises part of my job and other things we'll bring up at a later time."

"We?"

"Remember, Luzi, you are all of this: the human, the I Am, the Gnost, the Master Wisdom and me. We are all you!"

I feel overwhelmed as a touch of this truth once again rolls over me. "The true oneness!"

I sense Knight nodding, and then he brings forth the next subject. "When talking about guilt, we must also talk about forgiveness. As we all, especially Saint Germain, have told you numerous times, right and wrong is part of the duality game and has no connection to the I Am, which has no judgement at all. The conclusion should be that if there is no judgement, then there is no right and wrong and then there is no need for forgiveness."

"But at the human level it is pretty much all about judgement of some kind. It is totally real to the human entity."

"Yes, that is why the human part of you must receive forgiveness for what it sees as things it has done wrong. The mind, which is really what we are talking about here, cannot forgive itself, because it knows, in its judgemental state, that what it has done is wrong. It knows; it can't fool itself into believing in self-forgiveness."

I can see where Knight is going with this. "So, what you say is that to release the guilt, the mind must receive forgiveness from the highest authority it knows, the divine!"

Knight smiles. "Exactly, Luzi. Your human part must receive forgiveness from the I Am, but the hurdle is: Does it feel it is worthy to receive this forgiveness? The I Am will grant this forgiveness as many times as it takes because there is nothing to forgive, but is the human REALLY ready or willing to receive it? That's the tricky part, indeed."

I can see that even if a person so desperately searches for forgiveness, its lack of self-esteem, the lack of worthiness, might block it.

"So, the issue is really about self-esteem and feeling worthy to receive forgiveness; being forgiven is the easy part."

"Yes, the question to anyone who asks for forgiveness is: Can you REALLY RECEIVE FORGIVENESS?"

I nod and let this statement sink in. "The person must have a deep feeling of readiness and state: I RECEIVE FORGIVENESS! That's the only way. At the same time, I know the human doubt is powerful, and it comes from the mind as well as the longing for forgiveness, as well as the voice that comes with all kinds of excuses for NOT BEING GUILTY. It really sucks!"

"It sucks, as you say. That is why a lot of clearing must be done BEFORE a person truly can receive the gift of forgiveness."

I feel moved as this strikes a string of truth deep inside me.

"When you say, the GIFT of forgiveness, I truly hear you say that there is nothing to forgive, but the gift is still given, because that is what the human needs."

Knight starts to get up, so I get up as well. He stretches his legs and gently shakes his wings.

"Can I offer you a sightseeing flight around the area, dear?"

"Oh yes! Loong and Shaumbra have shown me the near surroundings and Elvendale City from above, but I have never been taken further out over the sea and inland over the mountains and huge woodlands."

Knight gets down on his belly again, and I use his front leg as a staircase to find a place just behind his neck. I find a perfect spot to sit without risking falling off. Not that I imagine I would ever do so in Elvendale. Things are different here.

From the top of the volcano we fly over the lake, follow the river to the sea, crossing the low mountains that shield the freshwater lake from the saltwater of the sea. I see the bench where Saint Germain and I recently enjoyed the sunrise. The sea is calm, seen from up here anyway, and the white and blue sails of fishing vessels dot the green-blue surface. Large whales play in the deep waters. The beluga or white whales are easy to spot. Small ones like dolphins join people in the shallow waters near the coast. Some people waves at us, and Knight makes a tight downward loop to get closer to them before he continues inland, crossing the lower highland from where we started. Close to the city, these hold the farmland of the community. He continues over the vast grasslands dotted with lakes and small streams and we reach the outskirts of the enormous forest of which I could not see the end. I see it is not only dense forest, but there are a lot of clearings and less dense forestation.

I have lost track of time because there is so much to sense, not only see. This brief flight could have taken a whole afternoon to complete had it been done in 3D. Knight is the third dragon I have ridden and I am excited with joy. Knight turns and we fly towards Elvendale City, where he sits down in the centre of the round plaza in the middle of the city; if you can use the word *middle*, because the city covers most of a mountain top.

From my position on the beautiful dragon, I recognise my good and first friend in Elvendale, Josela, coming towards us. I wave at her, slide down and kiss Knight on the cheek while looking into his beautiful eyes, which continue to fascinate me.

"Thank you for everything, Knight. I feel it is time for a mug of tea, maybe some cinnamon cookies or a raisin roll and some girl talk."

"Indeed, but we will soon meet again, dear Luzi."

Josela looks lovely as she always does. Her sleeveless dress is thin. It could be red silk and reaches just below her knees. Her dark hair is loose, but still with a red ribbon in it.

"Tea and a raisin roll AND, not or, cinnamon cookies will suit me fine. I know exactly where to find those goodies!"

First, she walks to Knight and takes his big head between her hands and kisses him loudly on the snout.

"Hello, Knight. So, you have aired the princess. She is not green in the face, so you went gently with her, I guess!"

"I wouldn't scare her off during the first flight with me! We might take it up a few notches next time. I can be quite scary, you know."

Josela smiles. "You're the gentlest of the gentle!"

Knight takes off and flies out of sight behind the buildings above us.

The ageless woman turns to me, we hug and then she takes my hands in hers and looks me in the eyes. "My dear, dear Luzi. You look gorgeous. Let's get some tea and gossip!"

"Thanks, Josela. You look wonderful and timeless, as always. A new dress, I guess?"

"Oh, I made it a few minutes ago when I sensed you would land here. I was at the beach gathering tiny sea shells for decorations. I saw you flying by."

She takes my hand and leads me to the edge of the plaza, which is surrounded with small shops and workshops. I put my other hand to my forehead.

"Oh, I forgot how easy it is to create here in Elvendale. I'm wearing a blue dress like the last time I was with Knight here."

"Blue suits you; it goes well with the colour of your eyes. Here we are. Take a seat."

There are tables and chairs outside a small café. Even though the sun is high in the sky, the light and the warmth are not overwhelming, so there is no cover above us and we can enjoy a vast view of the inlands. We see the mountains, the green highlands with the long bridge leading into the city, and the forest farthest off behind the farmland.

I pick a chair close to the plaza, and Josela takes a place where we both can see the plaza and at the same time look at each other as we talk. I choose a spicy chai which has much more flavour than the ones in my 3D world. Josela chooses a green tea with mostly lemon and honey. She also orders raisin rolls—she shows four fingers—and cinnamon cookies from the young waiter. I can see he enjoys his job; there is no acting here. He returns with butter and a basket containing the rolls and cookies. It has a cloth cover, so the bread keeps warm.

"Ladies! The tea comes in a few moments!"

Shortly after, he returns with our tea and small jars with different jams. As I taste the first roll, I understand why Josela has ordered four of them.

While watching the life unfolding in the plaza, Josela and I talk about her "jobs" and what she has been up to lately, and I tell about my family and our new life in Hastings. I also mention my grandma in Hong Kong and our trip in the autumn to meet her for the last time.

Julia's first birthday

A week after my visit in Elvendale, Ju-long's mother Ting and her husband Cheng arrive at Heathrow Airport west of London. It is Monday, very early, and Dad picks them up. He takes them to Mum and Dad's home in Sevenoaks where they will stay until Wednesday, when they drive down to us in Hastings to celebrate Julia's first birthday, which is 6 May 2020. I assume my sister Anna will be with them as well. She prefers Dad's car to the train, so she will only take the train from London to Sevenoaks. He still has his copper-coloured Tesla X with seven seats. It had an update recently, so it runs better than ever, Dad says.

Some weeks ago, we visited Mum and Dad in their wonderful house in Sevenoaks. Here we found out that Julia was very fond of the grand piano in the large living room. Now her grandparents have made it her birthday present this year. I argued that she doesn't have the motor skills to actually play it, but Dad argued that if the grand piano wasn't in her home, she wouldn't have the opportunity to play her way into actually playing it, and we have lots of space in our living room. I couldn't argue against that, so this morning, her birthday, a large truck shows up delivering the grand piano. The men use a narrow, motorised cart to transport the large instrument right into our living room, where they assemble it. The transport company is a family business, and the eldest man, the founder, handed Julia the birthday card from her grandparents. After the truck has left, we all read the card and Julia is very excited.

Earlier this morning, Ju-long and I were up finishing what we had prepared in the evening, before we walk into Julia, singing a birthday song.

Julia is quick to get up and joins the song. We sit on the floor where she opens her presents, assisted by the two cats. The presents from us are a gipsy dress with the base colour being yellow, and beige sandals. After this: PANCAKES, yeah! She knows about the pancakes, because that was what she ordered last evening before bed, and the smell was all over the place, impossible to hide. The cats get a small pancake each, served by Julia, after they have finished the raw turkey meat slice.

After breakfast, Julia wants a bath in the bathtub. "No cats!" she says and points to shoo the cats away. They go outside to their secret lives of which no ordinary human knows. Julia spends not too much time in the bathtub, because she wants to get ready and wear her new dress and sandals before the guests arrive. She is ready just as the truck with the grand piano stops in front of the house.

The truck leaves, and Ju-long sits with her on his knee at the piano while she hits the keys. Suddenly she stops and turns her head to the entrance. "Granddad!"

We all look out of the window, but can't see the Tesla. Julia wants to get down, so Ju-long places her on the floor. She runs to the glass door leading to the entrance. Now we see the copper-coloured car turn onto the driveway. Julia and Dad surely have a special connection.

Ju-long runs to the door which opens to the entrance and then to the outside. Somehow Dad was the first out of the car and receives Julia kneeling and with open arms. It is so moving to see. I follow them outside, and now there is a lot of hugging and smiling, and all admire Julia and her new outfit.

We all walk inside, and Julia takes Mum's hand to show her or thank her for the grand piano.

"Yes, Julia. Granddad and I wanted to give you the piano, because it is great for expressing oneself."

People drag their bags and suitcases inside and we show them where they will sleep. Mum and Dad use the large bathroom, and their stuff goes in a locker in the connection area.

Ting and Cheng sleep in our study, Anna with Julia and the cats, and Mum and Dad in the living room, testing the new sofa which is also a comfortable double bed.

I wonder if we have built our house too small. We could have chosen a sixty-foot ground diameter dome or had our fifty-foot diameter made with two floors. A baby boy will probably show up next year as well to demand his space.

I sense Julia gently shaking her head and smiling. "Dear Luzi, Mum. Just add a floor above all the rooms except the living room and kitchen, then there will be plenty of space for the growing family."

The last part she says with a twinkle, and I am not quite sure what to think. I am sure the family will not grow larger than her younger brother when he shows up at some point in the future. Well, what she really means is that I can take it easy. All will form well in the years to come.

Ju-long and I had not had the time to arrange a brunch, but everyone does their part. Anna, Ting and Julia set the table, Cheng and I do most of the rest, and Ju-long and Dad make rolls, cinnamon rolls and other bread from the dough Ju-long made yesterday, and, after an hour or so, we are ready.

Dad has brought sweet oranges and a few lemons for the orange presser, and a joint of lamb will go into the oven after brunch. I look forward to some wonderful days with not too much planned.

After brunch, Julia and Anna take a nap. The rest of us clean up before Ting and Cheng get a tour inside the house. When we are back in the living room with Mum and Dad, I tell them about Julia's suggestion about a second floor. Dad is much surprised, but he thinks we can do it.

"You must talk to Jacob and the others, because there is much more than just a floor and walls that need to be added."

Shortly after, I hear Anna and Julia talking.

"I have a very special present for you, Julia. It is large and we must work to put it together. The present is over at Jacob's, and he will help to get it over here. It is a sandbox for your playground. The first thing we'll put there."

"We go to Jacob. He's nice!"

"Yes, let's get some outdoor things on and find Jacob!"

They come into the living room on their way out. Julia is very excited. "Anna and I will build a sandbox."

It surprises us that Julia speaks an entire sentence flawlessly. Cheng shows his excitement too.

"Can I watch when you are building it, Julia?"

"All can watch and help!"

Mum is astounded at her granddaughter's abilities, being just a one-year-old.

"She surely has her meaning about things and

knows how to express it!"

Ju-long smiles. "And I can't even say: of course, with those parents! Because she is her very own."

The two girls wear "working clothes" now. Jacob lives next door, so they only have to make a brief walk. A little later we see them coming. Jacob has a large two-wheeled barrow on which the wooden parts lie wrapped in plastic. Julia and Anna walk right behind him, hand in hand.

I can't believe it is my ONE-YEAR-OLD daughter. It is as if she has turned the maturity gauge a few steps up this very morning. I mean, ONE YEAR. Ju-long takes my hand. He feels the same.

"Well, let's see how we can help. Jacob and I have planned it out, but didn't want to do anything with the area beforehand. All tools and accessories are ready."

I will spare you the details, but will tell you that everyone is involved in the construction. When the sandbox is ready, Jacob and Julia pick up sand from under a tarpaulin, from the supply area where we get most of the common materials to be used in the village. Julia sits in the barrow both ways, enjoying it immensely. I can see Jacob is enjoying it as well.

Jacob tilts the sand into the sandbox which has already been made weather-resistant. He puts down the barrow and kneels in front of Julia, who gives him a long hug.

"Thanks, Jacob. See you!"

"See you, princess!"

The big man has tears in his eyes as he gets up from the kneeling position and he smiles. "Such a small puppy can turn a grown man to tears!"

We wave goodbye as the big man pushes the wheelbarrow, following the swirling garden path to the pavement.

Anna fetches a net with toys to use in the sandbox, and then she and Julia stay outside playing, while the rest of us clean up or go inside to prepare a substantial afternoon tea.

When tea is ready, Ting walks outside to ask Anna and Julia to come in. The toys stay in the sandbox, and Anna shows Julia how to put the lid over it to prevent animals from using the sandbox as a toilet.

Inside, Anna gives Julia a clean nappy and they are both dressed up for the birthday party to continue now they arrive at the tall table. Ting has made a layer cake, and she carries it in from the kitchen with its one candle lit. We sing the birthday song. Anna is ready to help Julia blow out the candle, and we are all surprised that Julia does it on her own.

She talks to me non-verbally. "This was one of my physical goals for my one-year birthday. That's why you have seen a huge leap in my abilities."

After the tea, there are still presents for Julia. This time from Ting and Cheng. I hear the cat door slap and Boomer and Snow join in to help with the unwrapping. It is mostly the wrapping paper and the laces that interest them. Julia discovers some cat's ear hair clips, a potty with cats for when it comes time to use it, a tepee larger than the normal children's tepee, and beautiful clothes handcrafted in Hong Kong.

Mum had to comment on all the clothes while looking at me. "With all those clothes you should have another girl. I guess Julia will outgrow them quickly!"

I smile. "Well, I have been told there are other plans in that matter. No dresses will go there!"

"Oh, I look forward to that, dear!"

"Well, I hope it's not right around the corner."

Anna says in fun, "Oh, if it's too much for you, can I have him then?"

Ju-long doesn't want to be left out of the discussion, since he will be part of it. "Oh Anna, I know you'll be a perfect mother, but this one will stay with us. Babysitting will be allowed, though!"

After tea, Ting and Chan take Julia outside to set up the tepee on the lawn. Dad assures us that the lawnmower for this area will avoid the tepee, even without reprogramming it. We will take the tepee inside in the evening, so there is no problem there.

The rest of us clean up after tea and prepare to go outside as well.

Blueberry

I am the first to walk outside and head for the tepee. I can hear Julia and Anna talking inside it. From the corner of my eye I see a large bird approaching, and when I look up, I think it is a crow trying to land on the top of the tepee. The sunlight is in my eyes, so I can only see the bird's shape and wonder about the long tail. The bird lands and grasps hold one of the poles sticking out of the top of the tepee. I am closer now and can see it is a parrot; totally blue. That is strange. I whisper to the girls in the tent.

"Girls, come out slowly. There is a parrot sitting at the top of the tepee!"

I stand completely still, so as not to scare the bird away.

Julia comes out first. "Hi, bird. I am Julia!"

The parrot responds in the typical parrot voice. "Hi, good afternoon!"

Anna's head pokes out of the tepee. She looks up and whispers, "Wow, a talking parrot!"

I can sense the rest of the family standing a little away in awe of the scene.

Julia sits down on the grass and the bird glides down and lands near her and walks the rest of the way to her. It obviously doesn't want to scare her. The bird is huge, especially compared to Julia. They seem to have the same height. Julia reaches out one hand to invite the bird to approach further.

Anna crawls out and sits next to Julia. She has all her attention on the big strong bird. Julia touches the feathered chest, and the bird doesn't move. I walk up to them and sit down on the other side of Julia. Anna takes out her phone, starting to film us. I can see Julia and the bird are very focused on each other. It feels very intense. I talk in a low voice. "Where do you come from, dear?"

The bird totally ignores me. Now Julia opens both arms and invites the parrot in for an embrace. I really have to fight myself not to take action, but from previous situations I know Julia can handle it. The blue bird steps up to Julia and puts its cheek to Julia's and she gives it a gentle hug that lasts a few seconds. Then the bird takes a step back. Julia's little body moves in excitement.

"Good bird!"

The parrot replies. "Good bird!"

Ju-long comes and sits next to me, and Mum, Dad, Cheng and Ting sit down behind us. The scene is totally surreal. Suddenly the bird turns its head to me, fixating me with one eye surrounded with a small ring of yellowish skin. The skin also shows at the inner edge of the lower beak.

"Lovely cookies!"

It gets me thinking of the cinnamon cookies in El-vendale.

"I may have some inside. Do you want a cookie?"

"Lovely cookies! Good bird!"

I guess it means yes, so I slowly turn my back to the bird, get up and walk inside to choose a cookie jar, the contents of which may be in the bird's taste. I take out one cookie, put on the lid and hide the jar behind me as I walk out to sit in my place beside Julia. The bird follows my movements, and I reach out my hand with the cookie.

"Here is a cookie!"

With its beak, the blue parrot gently picks the cookie out of my hand, not snapping it, as I would have expected. Now it holds it with one claw, breaks a small piece off it and eats it. I can see the odd bird's tongue moving around the cookie bite.

"Lovely cookies!"

"You're welcome. Where do you come from?"

"Good bird!"

"Yes, you're a good bird! What is your name?"

"Good bird!"

I turn to Ju-long. "We must announce the bird. It obvious belongs to someone. It can't have appeared out of nowhere!"

He takes a picture with his phone and sends it to the village's forum on the Internet, and then he returns his focus to us.

"I also sent it to the Hastings Community. It may have flown far."

I hear Dad from behind. "It should have some water. I'll fetch some."

Mum gets up as well. "Oh, what about the cats? They may find the bird too interesting!"

Shortly after, Dad comes back with a bowl of water.

"Here is some water for our blue friend!"

He places the bowl in front of Ju-long before he sits down next to him. He reports on the cats. "The cats are slumbering away in the tree in the living room. Mum's keeping an eye on them."

The parrot has finished the cookie and looks at the water. "Thanks, dear!"

Then it puts its beak into the water and drinks. "Lovely!"

Ju-long smiles. "It certainly has some vocabulary."

He looks at the bird again. "It will soon be dark. I suggest you fly home. Fly home!"

The bird indicates that it heard him. "Fly home."

"Yes, fly home. Goodbye bird."

"Good bird! Lovely cookies!"

"Hm, it wants to fill its belly before taking off, I guess."

Ting, who sits behind me, silently picks up a cookie from the jar and puts it in my hand which I hold behind my back. I put the cookie in Julia's hand.

"Last cookie, then you fly home!"

Julia hands out the cookie and the parrot carefully picks it from her hand, as it did from mine before. Then, holding the cookie in one claw, it breaks off a small piece with its beak and hands it back to Julia.

"Lovely cookies!"

Julia picks the piece from the beak and eats it. After this, the parrot picks another piece and eats it itself. The third piece goes to Julia and so it goes on until Julia gets the last one. Then the parrot drinks some water and takes off, first landing on the top of the tepee, then at the top of one of the small trees in the garden. It begins to tend its feathers. Julia gets up and waves to the bird.

"See you!"

While not interrupting the grooming, the parrot replies. "See you!"

We all get up and I pick up Julia. If we all go inside, the bird might lose interest and fly home.

"Soon the bird will fly home."

Anna looks at her phone. "I just ran out of battery. I must recharge before I can send you the video. It was so strange … and beautiful!"

Back inside, Ju-long finds out that the parrot is a hyacinth macaw. It is a beautiful and intelligent bird and I hope it finds its way back home.

We start preparing dinner. Dad puts the joint of lamb in the oven, and vegetables and other stuff are being prepared. Ju-long makes dough for flutes, which will go into the oven when the roast lamb is finished. When we are all occupied in the kitchen, I hear Julia laugh in her room and walk in to check on her.

She sits in the middle of the room with Boomer, Snow and the parrot, all having a good time! I sneak out and call the others. I ask Ju-long to take his phone to record the scene. When we reach the door, I hear Anna whisper, "WHAT? How did it come in?"

Dad has the answer. "One of the automatic windows must have been open. It is warm in the house and it is better to use the natural ventilation than the cooling system."

Ting whispers a question. "What should we feed the thing, if we have to keep it until we hear from its owner?"

I take a picture of the group and post it together with the question on what to do while the bird is with us.

This is a summary of what came back: It must always have access to fresh water. Feed it twice a day. Small amounts of fruits, vegetables, grains, and seeds. Pellets, which is a combination of these things. Nuts, legumes, cooked meat like chicken. NO avocados or chocolate. There was no advice about checking its gender other than a DNA test, which I later found out on the Internet.

What about a cage or box? We can't just have a large bird flying free around in the house. Cheng comes up with a solution that may work.

"The bird may find the tree in the living room attractive. Why not make a platform for it, but take into account where it puts its droppings? I suppose the cats wouldn't steel the food. You may start with putting a cookie on the platform to show it the way. The sleeping platform can be high up, but below the cats so it doesn't dump its droppings on them. The feeding platform may be low enough that you can reach it from the floor."

We have most of the foods for the parrot, but raisins must take the place of pellets, and Cheng and Julong begin creating the platform, so it is ready for the night. It amazes us that the cats don't fight the parrot, but, as we observe the three, it seems that we should be more worried about the cats, which put up with the parrot's grooming and nudging.

Julia contacts me, teaching me a little, I guess. "Why make such a fuss out of this? The bird will find a place to sleep and you can place something to catch its droppings under it. Put the feeding bowls next to the cats' bowls. You'll soon find out what you can place beside the cats' dry food. You can feed the rest in the morning and the evening, when you feed the cats. Three bowls in a row. The fountain provides the water."

"Thanks, Julia. Is there something else I should know?"

"Well, not for the moment. You must learn to use your own discernment."

I find the men to stop the project and tell them about Julia's suggestions. Now we look forward to seeing how the feeding will go.

Coming back to the living room, I see our FOUR kids playing at the fountain in the junction area. The parrot seems to like playing with the water as much as the others. Julia is laughing loudly.

We feed the animals just before we get to the dinner table and it works out fine. Cats and bird are interested in each other's food, but eventually they stick to their own bowls. So far, so good. After eating, the cats take to their favourite spots in the tree, and the large bird settles down on a thick branch as well. I notice there are no obstacles between the bird and the floor; excellent. I just hope this will be THE spot and place a large salver with some paper on the top to catch the droppings.

Later I check the bird's bowl and find that raisins are left so we can use them as equivalent to the cat's dry food. We can get some pellets tomorrow.

During dinner, Dad asks Julia if she would like to visit the public swimming pool tomorrow as an extra birthday present with him and her grandma. Others might join as well. He gets a loud and clear

YES in response. We already knew the answer, since she loves water and swimming.

Later this evening, after Ting has tucked Julia in, the cats go out on their evening adventure. I keep an eye on the parrot, but it stays on the branch. Later it checks the fountain again, the food bowls, and then it checks on Julia. The door to the room is ajar, and it silently walks in. I sneak up and look through the crack. It checks Julia in her bed and the Boombox before it walks out again. One more time to the fountain to clean up before bed and then it flies up to its branch. A little more grooming before it puts its head under its wing. I guess I can get used to having this beautiful, intelligent and magnificent bird in my home.

The next morning, Thursday 7 May, I get up early to take a shower before the others get up, but first I check on the parrot. It sits on its branch, but flies down, landing on the back of a chair at the dinner table.

"Lovely cookies!"

"Oh, you want breakfast. Could you wait until I'm out of the shower, then you can eat together with the cats?"

"Nice bird!"

"Yes, you are a nice bird. I'll be back at once."

I walk to the small bathroom we use with Julia, but when I have the door fully open, the parrot flies in, landing on Julia's changing table.

"Nice bird!"

"Well, if you are a nice bird, you stay there until I have finished. OK?"

"Nice bird!"

I get behind the shower curtain and adjust the water temperature before stepping under the showerhead.

"Peek-a-boo!"

A blue head peeks in under the shower curtain, and then the big blue parrot walks into the shower. There is no doubt the bird likes the water. Another water-crazy family member has joined our flock. I don't want to get soap on the bird, so after a short while I clap on the tap to encourage it to fly up there. It is a tight space, but the bird manages to land and get a grip on the smooth metal. I hurry to finish, then shut off the water and pull away the curtain. I point out of the shower.

"We're done. I need to dry myself. How about you?"

"Nice bird!"

It shakes its body and water drops flies all over.

"Oh, I see you can do that yourself."

I can hear cats outside the bathroom door. Oh, more animals who want a morning shower. Well, that must wait until later today. I wrap a towel around my hair and put on my dressing gown. As I open the door, I shoo away the cats, get the bird out and close the door. Phew. Next step, feeding time.

"Come, kitties, breakfast."

The parrot flies to its branch and I take out frozen slices of salmon for the cats, which I thaw in cold water. They are thin slices, so it only takes a few minutes. The cats are watching me work. Now I measure food for the parrot and put it in a bowl. I can hear flapping wings. It learns fast!

Finally I can get dressed. I meet Dad on my way to the bedroom.

"Oh, you're up early, dear!"

"Yes, I wanted to get a shower before anyone, you in particular, got up. But guess what? The parrot took a shower with me and it really enjoyed it!"

Dad laughs. "At least you don't have to brush and groom it like you have to do with the cats! By the way, why shower when we're driving to the pool later this morning?"

"Well, actually I forgot about the pool, or I was not all awake, or the parrot hypnotised me to do so! I guess I just needed a shower and got up and took one."

"Well, if you hadn't, I might have been the lucky

one taking a shower with the blue parrot."

Yesterday and today we get a lot of responses on our announcement about the parrot, but no one claims it.

It seems the blue parrot becomes a part of the family, and at the breakfast table I ask Julia what we should call it. Mostly in fun, because I did not expect her to answer me in words, but to our surprise it came loud and clear.

"Blueberry."

Then she laughs out loud. I assume the human part and the soul/consciousness have something going on.

Julia communicates to us nonverbally. "There is really no difference between me, the soul and the wisdom and the human mind. You may say, I don't have a human mind nor the Master Wisdom. They have been woven into ME. Now the Gnost has replaced my mind and wisdom, but I rely on the woven-in parts when I socialise with people and act in the outer world. I keep the appearance of my Free Energy Body in an almost normal development phase, not to draw too much attention from the officials, but that will change after the two-year check, after which there are no mandatory checks. No-one in the family uses baby-talk with me. I don't think anyone should use baby-talk to any child, because how can a child learn how to speak correctly if it doesn't hear normal spoken language? In the beginning, the sentences should be short, but children are quick to pick up the code. It is the speaking ability that is delayed, not the understanding of what is spoken, but they may not understand every word."

Ju-long has a question for her. "But you just spoke the name, Blueberry, loud and clear, like you did some of your talking yesterday?"

Julia again answers nonverbally. "I produced a single word or a brief sentence and at the same time pointed at the word in your mind or memory. I will not speak to you the way I do now, while my body is so young. It will feel unnatural for both you and me, especially because it's not baby-talk."

I need her to elaborate on this. "How do you feel about being an adult and having the body of a small child and people treating you as a small child?"

"Oh, that doesn't bother me at all. I always meet people at their level of consciousness, or you may call it common understanding in the dialogue. I read or sense them at all levels and may seed understandings that fit their system, which may sink into their awareness at some point. You must understand that a human is a child no matter the age. It may have gained experiences and even wisdom, but the human part and psyche is still built on a child. I will even say that the I Am or what people call the soul IS a child. Well, even simpler than a child, because the soul has NO needs and NO judgement. Think of Julia simply enjoying the moment of sheer joy."

It is still difficult for us to see the full picture of what Julia is and how she works, but I guess it prepares us for the second child whom I have briefly touched upon as consciousness to consciousness.

Ju-long brings up an issue we both have thought about, namely potty training. Julia has a prompt response.

"I really don't care about doing it in the nappy. It is just a condition, and I wouldn't let it influence the body's skin. Because I have no ego, I don't judge the situation. When my body can hold or accumulate the waste, we'll start with the potty."

I can see that the next challenge we face will be the teenage period, but before I can form a sentence and say it, Julia answers me.

"Don't worry Mum. There wouldn't be any hormones neither an ego to act out."

After afternoon tea, Ju-long and Dad do some shopping to supplement our food supply. The rest of us simply enjoy the afternoon sunshine coming through the windows, adding a warm glow to the interior of the dome house. Julia, Boomer, Snow and Blueberry entertain us. Julia shortens the large parrot's name to just Blue. Three pets and three colours, orange, white and blue. Sarah pays us a brief visit, spending most time with the children. We can see her approaching through the glass areas at the entrance and I notify Julia who runs to the front door. After hanging up her coat and taking off her boots, she comes into the living room with Julia on her arm.

"I was on my way home when I felt the urge to drop in. I guess Julia wants to show me the new family member. Everyone in the village is talking about it. Snow is also part of the talk."

Julia points at the large bird which sits on the living room floor with the cats.

"Blueberry!"

"Wow, it is really huge! Almost as tall as you, Julia."

Julia and the animals had been playing with peanuts in shells, so when Sarah puts Julia on the floor, Blue walks over, handing Sarah a peanut.

"Good bird!"

"Thanks, Blue. You certainly are a good bird."

Sarah cracks the shell and eats the two nuts.

"Um, they're wonderful."

I can see Anna wants to join in on the group, but she stays on the sofa to let Sarah have her moments with the young ones. Sarah will babysit them all in the future. She leaves again when Dad and Ju-long come back from their shopping trip and we begin making dinner.

Every day, Ju-long and I update Julia's journal and copy some entries to an online journal at her nursery, Artemis. This way, they will know what she might communicate about when she stays there.

Days when Mum and Dad visit us, Julia stays with us. Because we have planned this visit well in advance, Ju-long and I can take these days off and do a few work-related things in the evening.

DNA and New Energy

In the night, Saint Germain visits me, and once again the subjects are the human DNA and energy. This time we hover above the arm of the Milky Way where our solar system is. When he tells me that there is only one energy, I get an initial thought or picture of this. We draw all "things" with the same pen, and both the pen, the ink and the paper are this one energy. I sense him smiling as he continues.

"When I say there is only one energy, I mean that you only have access to your own energy and there is no limit to it, other than what you, as a human, pretend it to be. There are not different types of energy, so your analogy about the pen, the ink and the paper fits perfectly."

There is much talk about DNA in new age materials, so I ask Saint Germain to clarify the basics of it.

"As life began on Earth, you had a thread or string of information to guide you how to live as a biological being on the planet. This way, you didn't have to learn everything all over when you returned for another lifetime."

I have never heard or read about this before. "So

this was the first DNA!"

"Yes, and it eventually became the first simple two-strand DNA."

Saint Germain tells me that both energy and DNA are vital in the life of each cell. "The body's old energy and light communication network, the Anayatron, distributed energy to all cells and information to and from the DNA in each cell."

Now he moves on to talk about my situation, as he had before. "New energy demands a new energy distribution system and changes in the DNA. With the Anayatron gone, a new communication system must be added. When your body gradually changes from being carbon based to being New Energy based, you will need no energy distribution system because the Free Energy Body IS energy, so no distribution is necessary."

"You've told me that energy comes from my I Am. Is that true for both the old and the new energy?"

"We can say that the so-called old energy you use on Earth is from when you left The Eternal One and gained self-awareness. The New Energy you are getting accustomed to derives from the joy of the I Am, your I Am, you. It is truly your own energy and you own it exclusively."

I sense there is more, so I nod to encourage him to continue, which he willingly does.

"The I Am creates the template, so to speak, for the creation, but it is through the human perception and experience that life is manifested. The I Am does not know these templates, which we may call the Pool of the Great Unknown. This is what the human dives into, making the energy come to life, and experiencing and perceiving this creation on behalf of the I Am and the Master.

"The human life attracts these templates according to the human's state of awareness and its capability to work with energy or really allow energy to work with you. As you use more of your true senses, of which we have talked before, the energy which we call New is much more active in both attracting blueprints and creating from them. When you truly step into this pool, you are free to discover everything in here. The true creator, which is really you as the I Am/Human unity, will be aware of this creation every moment of your life."

Now I need a short refresh of something the count has told me before. "You've mentioned that the human part is essential for the embodied realisation. Please tell me again why the I Am must have the human aspect in this respect."

"In a way, I just did. The human aspect will integrate in the I Am and become a facet which gives the I Am its perception of the world, making the energy come to life for creation, and bringing the experience from this life. Without experience, there will only be awareness for the I Am."

I create some visions in my mind, so I can bring this concept into my human world. "An aspect is a separate part of a whole, while the facet is an integrated part of a whole. An insect in a piece of amber is an aspect, while a plane surface of a diamond is a facet. The diamond isn't the same diamond without it. The facet cannot not be there."

Saint Germain sends me a thumbs-up. "A very good analogy, Luzi!"

It amazes me that we can keep on talking about these subjects and, every time we do, new things come up. I sense this "flight" above the Milky Way with Saint Germain is over when he poses me this question.

"You see why the human part is so important in this creation?"

"Yes, I do. Without the human, everything would still just be awareness, and that is what consciousness is. This creation would have been a waste of energy, said in human terms!"

I experience opening my eyes in my human bed, looking up at the ceiling and still looking down at the Milky Way galaxy. Now the stars fade away and Saint Germain bows as always before my focus turns to my human life.

The fishing cats

Today, Friday 8 May, Mum, Dad, Ting and Cheng will visit Wakehurst a one-hour-and-fifteen-minute drive to the north-west. Wakehurst is a botanic garden with over five hundred acres of plants from all over the world.

While "the old folks" visits Wakehurst, the rest of us, being Anna, Julia, Ju-long and I, visit the two water reservoirs in a small green area near Harold Road. We plan to get our lunch at our favourite Chinese take-away, New Hong Kong Kitchen, also on Harold Road. The Clive Vale Angling Club manages the two small lakes.

Because of much interest in the Dome Village from the surrounding population, our two cats are well known. "The cats that live in the igloo!" Now Blueberry adds to this.

As we approach a small grass area with Julia's pushchair and a few blankets, we see two elderly men standing at a platform next to the water with their fishing rods. They have their backs towards us, but turn around as they hear us.

"Oh hello, I'm Albert. You're the Wang family from the Dome Village, right?"

Ju-long puts down the bag he carries and walks up to the men. "I am Ju-long Wang. This is my daughter Julia Wang, her mother Luzi Cane and Luzi's sister, Anna."

They shake hands and Ju-long continues. "May we lay out our blankets here, away from the water, not to disturb the fish?"

The other man answers. "Oh, you don't disturb anyone, neither the fish nor us. We're just here to enjoy the pleasant weather today. I'm Brad, by the way."

I lift Julia out of the pushchair and we walk hand in hand up to the platform. Anna has already laid out the blankets and Julia's toys and joins us. We say hello to Brad and Albert, who had just reeled in his fishing line, supporting the rod on the railing.

"Did you know that your cats are fishing in the reservoirs?"

I must have look shocked, because he quickly continues. "It's no problem, miss. They fish mainly from the shore and take smaller fish, while we go for the premium ones. The white one is mostly in the learning stage, but he catches on, so to speak."

He laughs at his play on the word "catch".

Ju-long wants to be sure the men are not just being friendly. "Small fish are food for bigger ones, and I'm pretty sure the cats aren't throwing back their catch."

Brad assures us they are sincere. "That's true, but it has some entertainment value to see them fishing. In a sense, we share the same passion."

Albert adds to that. "And they're not here all the time. Well, nor are we."

Anna, with her vivid imagination, brings up an idea. "They could be members of the angling club! This will give you some compensation for their catches."

We all laugh, including Julia, who sits on my hip.

Anna is serious and continues. "You COULD take it to the board."

Albert and Brad look at each other, and Brad smiles. "Well, why not? Then we have an interesting point for the next board meeting."

Anna seems to have it all figured out. "It would be great if you had some pictures to add to the notice of the meeting."

Albert rubs his chin. "I guess we already have some. Some younger members took a few the other day. Maybe we could use one of those."

I would like to have the pictures too, so I give him my card, which includes my email address.

"We would very much like a copy of those pictures. Preferably in their original size."

"Certainly! We'll see to that!"

It pleases Anna how her idea develops. "Thanks then. We'll take a walk around the ponds and then return to our blankets."

At lunch, Ju-long picks up our ordered food. He returns with fried chicken with mixed vegetables and fried rice, prawn crackers and mini vegetable rolls.

While Anna, Julia and I sit on the blankets waiting

for Ju-long, Julia speaks to me with her inner voice. "I have decided to stop being breastfed if it is all right with you. My body does not need ANY food, and I eat for pure enjoyment. I can even use my imagination with the food and have almost the same experience as actually eating it."

I am surprised, because we have talked about having a nearly normal early childhood with Julia.

"Well, it must be entirely up to you, dear. I guess we can just say that you have lost interest in being breastfed. I assume breastmilk in a bottle is included."

"Thanks, Luzi. I know that being breastfed gives special intimate moments between child and mother, but we can still have these moments, both physical and sensual."

"I hear you call me Luzi instead of Mum and say sensual instead of energetic. I guess we can expect great changes soon."

"You birthed my physical body, and I started out with you and Ju-long's DNA—well, sort of—so you will always be my mum and dad. You're my human mother and your human name is Luzi, but the real you is neither, as you know. The human emotions are hormones/peptides playing ping pong with thought. We'll use our true senses when we dance together, I Am with I Am."

Ju-long arrives, and when we are sitting with our food, I tell him and Anna about my small talk with Julia. Anna is the first to react.

"It makes sense. Beside the intimacy, breastfeeding is impractical, and the closeness to Julia sounds as though it will intensify rather than diminish. I hope I don't sound cold."

Ju-long answers her. "No, Anna, we know what you mean. I'm not involved in this part of raising a child, so I totally go with Julia."

While eating, I observe the one-year-old baby girl, sitting on the blanket, her legs spread out, with a chicken drumstick in one hand and a carrot stick in the other. I so love her and she will always be my daughter, no matter DNA and her own energy. She starts a verbal conversation with Anna.

"Boomer's fishing!"

"I bet you already knew!"

"Boomer and I talk."

She takes another bite of the chicken drumstick. Luckily, her teeth are well underway.

"Snow grows fast."

"Yes, he's a male and will probably grow larger than Boomer."

"They are cat friends."

"Yes, it's good they have each other, so they can share real cat adventures together."

"Blue must have a bird friend. I can teach them

many words."

"Well, luckily Blue has you to talk with, and all of us. It is a very clever bird."

When we leave the fishing ponds, we head east, away from the city, passing through a small forest. Here we make a short stop to the Ecclesbourne Reservoir where Julia had her first meeting with ducks, which was a grand experience for Ju-long and I. After feeding the ducks here, we walk northwest, crossing a small field where Julia had her first encounter with a female fox. This was an even grander experience for her parents to witness. Anna knows the stories, and she talks to Julia about them. Julia finds no reason to comment on them. We continue north, crossing Barley Lane, and soon we reach number 111.

Knight and forgiveness

Lately, I have been breaking into tears even more than usual. Most of the time I find no apparent reason, neither outside nor inside, what you may call emotional. As I ask for the deeper reason, Knight invites me to join him in his lair.

I, as consciousness, find myself in a dark cave with the black dragon welcoming me, looking at me with his fascinating blue eyes. It is not a scary place, because I know it is my own darkness that resides here and I have taken ownership of it. The cave has some tiny holes in the ceiling where light beams, thin as threads, touch the floor, inviting one to follow them up through the ceiling.

"Welcome, Luzi, into what is currently a part of you, including myself. In here is the wounded aspects not yet turned into facets of your being. You have been in part of this world with me before."

The dragon turns its head towards a large wall in the cave that seems to hold a pond raised vertically like a huge screen. It shows some blurred dark-grey and brown video clips and I know they are scenes of situations that incarnations of my I Am have stored or hidden in this cave. I know that to be ONE, I must be ALL I AM.

"I weep for those aspects because of what seemed to be their terrible pain and suffering at the time. But it was just the limited view I had then that gave me this impression, and now I realise that this was just a minor part of the entire experience. I Am holding no judgement against any of them. I know it's not Luzi who had these experiences, but Luzi is ME, and a human must bring these human experiences home."

"Your tears, and the understanding you have now, invite these aspects home from being hidden and separated parts of you to be facets of your journey."

Knight turns his large head and looks me straight in the eyes of my consciousness. "Will you follow me into one scene by moving into the screen?"

"I will, but which one should I choose?"

The screen changes to show many small video clips, like icons or thumbnails on a computer.

"Feel into it and choose one. I will be right behind you."

I sense into some scenes, but they all feel equally important, if that is the right term to use. How will I select one? Then I focus on one, blink as if I had clicked or tapped on my computer, and I immediately fly over a barren landscape in almost complete darkness. It is as if different places below are loaded with different emotions, as if I was walking down a street with different restaurants serving different dishes. I see a cliff face lit up by a bonfire, and I change my course towards the cliff.

As I approach the place, I see human shadows moving on the cliff face like a two-dimensional theatre play. Hate, greed and immense fear bid me welcome to this cruel play around the bonfire. I become participant and spectator at the same time.

Slave traders. The only reason to give the chained people food and water is to get a good price. This is an ordered delivery. I know we will lose some before we reach our destiny to the north, so I have picked a surplus in numbers, even it took another day to round them up.

I will not provide too many details, but I will say that in this lifetime I grew up in a Christian society, so there is a grim imbalance between what I know to be right and what I do for a living. I know that God has created everything, and treating the Lord's creations with disrespect, to say it mildly, is a sin. Later in that life, I will experience some life-changing events that take me away from this line of work, but I cannot forgive myself for my deeds. Here, hovering above this life, not only this scene, I forgive the one I am at the bonfire, knowing that all participants on their soul level knew this potential before incarnating.

I sense Knight behind me and think we must visit other events too, but Knight brings me back to his lair.

"We don't have to bring every event through the human awareness, but we'll address different issues from time to time as your human part opens to them."

I leave the black dragon and find myself in the bathtub immersed in bathwater with salt, crying tears of relief.

It is Saturday and the last day of Cheng and Ting's visit with us. Tomorrow they will leave with Mum, Dad and Anna for Sevenoaks. From there, Ju-lung's mother and her husband will leave together with Anna in a hired car for London, where Anna will stay. Cheng and Ting will visit some of Cheng's friends and business partners before they leave on Monday night for Hong Kong.

Today we will have a picnic at the ruins of Hastings Castle, which Cheng would like to visit. When

William of Normandy, known as William the Conqueror, landed in England in 1066, he ordered Hastings Castle built. There are also the ruins of a monastery with a large arch.

I won't go into details about the castle visit, other than to say that we have a great time, with calm weather and a wonderful view of the still water in the Channel.

While preparing dinner, I notice Blue showing great interest in the work while sitting on the back of a chair at the dining table. I turn my focus on it and use my non-verbal voice.

"What gender are you, Blue?"

"Blue is a male, but I have no gender. I am known as Isis, but also by other names, and for being part of Mother Mary from the Christian faith as well as Eve from the Old Testament. I also had other names and titles in much older ages where I was simply The Mother or The Goddess."

"Oh, like the Goddess Marija Gimbutas writes about!"

"Yes, I am part of all female goddesses, including Artemis and Sekhmet, the latter connected through the cat Boomer here in this house. It is no coincidence that Julia attends the Artemis Nursery, even though the founder does not fully know this. I have been here with Earth from the very beginning. I work with The Kryon and the 11:11 entourage. I will still be here when Gaia has left."

I know The Kryon from my extensive research and find it interesting that the name comes up here.

"You say you have no gender, and of course you don't. You are consciousness, but I guess all see Isis as the ultimate female representation."

"Well, Isis is a role just like Adam is a role. I AM consciousness just like you, as you just stated. I am neither female nor male, feminine nor masculine."

Isis sends me the most wonderful "smile" and tears roll down my face.

A typical Isis figurine, often in blue/turquoise.

Julia and I set the dinner table, and Blue flies back to his platform in the tree placed over a tray that collects his droppings.

We have cooked corncobs, and Blue comes down from the tree, landing on the back of my chair, very interested in my corncob. I take the smallest one from the serving dish, wipe it dry and hand it to the bird. This might be the reason for the bird's interest in the cooking process earlier. The large bird flies off with its catch and lands on its platform in the tree. Here he picks off the seeds one by one. As with the cats, Blue has an animal part as well as the consciousness that experiences and acts through the entity. Now we have Boomer/Sekhmet, White/Seth and Blue/Isis. All deity names from Egypt, but their consciousness does not carry these names, nor do they connect solely to Egypt.

The next morning, we have the last meal together before our guests head north. To my surprise, Ting and Cheng have already started preparing the breakfast when I get up. Julia and Ting set the dinner table with things from Julia's pull cart; the easiest way for her to bring the stuff from the kitchen. Julia wears her yellow dress, has two yellow ribbons in the hair and walks bare-footed. Cheng works at the stove and the oven, and I see Anna has already prepared oranges for the juicer. Now she cuts fruit and vegetables.

"Good morning, everyone. What a surprise. It's usually Mum and Dad who get up early and prepare the breakfast."

I kneel and kiss Julia on both cheeks.

Ting places two pots of jam from the pull cart on

the table and explains. "Yes, we knew that, so we arranged with Ya and Carl that we would prepare this last breakfast before we leave. Julia must have heard us in the bathroom, because she approached us together with the cats as we came out. The cats are outside now. I guess it's still a little early for Blue."

I see Blue on his platform, still with his head under his left wing. He will come down when he hears us serve his and the cats' breakfast.

After breakfast, cleaning up and getting the last things packed, we all go for a walk around the village. We observe how the different plots are developing and greet people who are outside on this lovely sunny Sunday morning.

During the walk I sense no one wants to part, and we are in no hurry to return to the house and the Tesla waiting to take our guests to Sevenoaks. We know that next time we see Ting and Cheng will be in Hong Kong in November when we say our last goodbye to Grandma Jiang. Eventually, the walk around the village comes full circle, and Anna picks up the bottles with water and juice from the refrigerator.

There are some long hugs, and Ting doesn't hide her tears as she says goodbye to her granddaughter.

"My life was so dull for a long time, but then Luzi showed up and suddenly Julia. And not to forget how Kong reappeared in everyone's life, being the wise man I always knew he was."

Indeed, all our lives have greatly changed since I made the reconnection with Lu-long after seeing him again in the library on Hong Kong Island. I see now that it was the initial play for Julia to appear on the planet, and then things really picked up speed.

The black lion goddess Sekhmet

To begin this chapter, I have found this beautiful depiction of Sekhmet as a black lion goddess.

The black lion goddess Sekhmet.

It is interesting to notice that Sekhmet's left breast is larger and hangs lower than the right one. Her stomach is not mirrored left to right either. I have seen a lot of mirrored stonework in and from Egypt. It is a mystery how this was achieved to such a perfection. This is not to say that Sekhmet was a real living being with a human body and a lion's head, but by portraying her this way it is much easier to imagine her as a living entity.

Since I met Knight in the moonlight experiencing MY so-called darkness, I have been wondering why the concept of dark and light has such a huge hook in peoples' psyche.

On a quiet afternoon when I work alone in the house, I sense Elvendale and Sekhmet, but I have no visual experience of either.

Sekhmet communicates in the non-verbal language of knowingness, where I KNOW what she "says".

"You surely remember the first time you met Josela in Elvendale."

"Oh, yes!"

"Elvendale is an actual place, and through this checkpoint you connect to my I Am, ME, and not specifically to Sekhmet, Bastet, Isis, Hathor and the others. These have mostly become human creations which are in the collective belief pool, which most of those who are even aware of such a thing call mass consciousness."

She is right, of course. Sekhmet is just a label I put on this consciousness when I sense it. I know I only sense a minuscule "part" of it. I move on with my question, knowing Sekhmet already knows it.

"Why is so-called darkness and evil associated with the colour black? I have seen numerous black or dark statues of Sekhmet."

"Oh, this came to be when the religions wanted to win over the pagans. The warm colours, red, orange and yellow, not only black, were associated with Earth, the spirit of Earth, the Mother of all things. You know that people have always used and even mined different materials with the ochre colour."

A picture comes to my mind. "It is interesting to find a black Madonna, a black Mother Mary. This way, the Catholic church could direct the pagans to their TRUE mother, the mother of Christ."

Sekhmet gets down to business. "If you want to sell something AS good and right, you can create the opposite and scare people with it by telling them it is bad and wrong. The pagan belief was often practised in dark caves representing the Mother's vulva, so there is much symbolism here, like Heaven and Earth, light and dark."

I sense Saint Germain raising a hand in the wings, knowing that religion is one of his passionate subjects.

The lie about the darkness

Saint Germain likes to act, so he shows up dressed like a priest, talking in a serious voice as the self-righteous priest would, but with words with a different meaning.

"Darkness is just a belief. It takes a choice to walk away from it. A bold step, because you must leave it one hundred percent, and there can be no negotiation with your doubtful mind. Move beyond the lies of darkness and step into freedom.

"Religions are invested in the lies of darkness, and they seldom talk about freedom, true freedom. You have done nothing bad, because there truly is no bad. There is no good either, for that matter.

"Walk on from the lie of darkness, power and that you have done something wrong. This is just part of the belief system imposed by those who are invested in power to control the rest.

"Freedom is when you allow that you have never done anything wrong."

Saint Germain enjoys the act immensely, but he puts it away, and I sense another subject coming up; and, sure enough, the subject changes.

BON

Saint Germain has changed into his professor costume, which is a black robe and headdress, a white shirt and tie and a crimson silk scarf. There is no podium, but he has a pointer which sends out a blue light beam like a laser pointer, which usually uses red light.

"I will introduce you to the term BON. You may find out later why I call it BON and write it in capital letters. We have talked about how the human brain translates the limited human awareness to play out what I called reality-projections. These projections appear on your BON screen. Instead of watching a play on your television, the human is in the play, and the I Am is watching AND experiencing the play through the human at the same time. Each of the other humans in the play have their own BON, and the common BON or collective BON screen overlays it all."

The professor continues and includes energy in the talk. "You can only perceive your own energy, so ALL you sense is your energy. YOUR energy is projected on the BON screen to be perceived."

"How about other people and our common experiences?"

"You may describe the world people perceive as being outside of themselves for Mass BON. It is a Common-Agreement-BON which each person perceives through their own BON. This was created during the Atlantis era to be the oneness of all Atlanteans. You can pull out your BON because it should be sovereign. You can always focus on the Mass BON if you want to and return to your BON when that feels right for you. After your realisation and embodied awareness, there is no subject/object because you ARE the I Am with the human vessel in the play AND outside the play, all by choice."

"This could make me feel quite alone in the world. I don't have direct contact with anybody. I am totally alone on my side of the BON. I can't even see another being, but only perceive their energy through my energy. It is like the human nervous system where signals through the eyes are being processed into images in the visual cortex."

"Well, yes. It is really no different from a normal human view of perceiving its world. You can't be sure that what you sense is actually what is in the 3D world. The knowledge of the BON should not make you feel more alone than your human self has ever felt."

I feel I need this BON thing to settle in and I change the subject with my next question. "We have talked about time before. I believe you said that there isn't even any now moment when everything happens. Could you please talk a little about that again?"

"When using the term the NOW moment, people still try to put things into a kind of time reference. They even call it the now MOMENT, which surely indicates that they are talking about time. Let us just take the timeline as an example and put a NOW-point on it. As soon as a so-called future event moves into the NOW-point, it becomes a past event. It simply can't sit in the NOW-point because there is no TIME for it to sit in."

"Good, I get it. In our 3D human reality, everything happens in the past. If I write a handwritten letter, in what I feel is the present moment or NOW, each line or stroke I make and which my eye can see must have been made in the past, or I wouldn't be able to see it."

"If that sets your mind at ease, this explanation is

as good as any."

He turns off the blue laser pointer, puts it in an inside pocket and straightens the crimson silk scarf. "This conclude the today's lecture and Q and A."

"Thank you, Professor!"

"Thank YOU, dear!"

Sekhmet gives me a warm hug before she fades away too.

William Li Wang

This morning I wake up with Boomer and Snow grooming at the foot of the bed, while Julia and Blue play hide-and-seek in the sheets on Ju-long's part of the bed. He must be making breakfast. I smile at all the life around me and can now feel the presence of my son-to-be. The touch is as always sweet and gentle as he sends me an ethereal smile. He has never appeared to any of us and shown us how he will look sometime in the future, as Julia did before she was born.

A white horse appears for my inner vision, bearing no rider, no prince in shining armour. We are on a hillside close to the edge of a forest of birch trees, and I am only a few yards from the grand horse, looking up at it. I reach out and touch the fair skin.

"You show up as a horse, dear?"

"Hmm, I Am the horse and I Am the rider. I can be seen and yet I Am invisible."

"A little cryptic, right?"

"Well, I could show up as a human figure, but I am less a human than I Am a horse."

"Have you chosen your human name as Julia did?"

"Nah, but William would be fine. It was your grand-dad's name. It also contains the Chinese name, Li."

"So, it could be William Li Wang?"

"It could."

"When can I expect you to be a physical part of the family?"

"I guess we will stay with Julia's wishes for that event."

"So, that means next year, 2021. At least nine months, right?"

"I can choose not to be birthed by you, but to appear into Earth reality being any age."

"That will certainly look strange to people around the family, not to mention the authorities; for example, if you show up as a five-year-old boy."

I sense Li smiling and feel a rush of love through my being.

"That will not be a problem. When I descend or expand myself onto the Earth realm, I lower a string of possibilities to this plane of existence. Even if they are not truly lived out, from other people's perspective the memories of me will be in their minds because of mass consciousness."

"So, I can suddenly have a five-year-old boy and NO ONE will question it, because they will KNOW I have this boy?"

"Yes! Cool, right? I'll even be in the records!"

"So, you manipulate the collective belief pool!"

"It kind of happens by itself when I pull in the possibility string. It's just energy, and energy is communication, or you could say information."

"Why didn't Julia do it that way. She seems eager to grow her body to adult size as quickly as possible?"

A moment passes. Then I can answer that question myself. "Because she CHOSE to do it the way she did!"

I sense a thumbs-up. Then he continues. "SAM came in to a shell body when it was around eight years old, if you remember. A body produced the old way. The connection with the I Am was done in a new way."

"Will I experience the pregnancy and your birth?"

"Because my human body is not grown, so to speak, you would have no true memory of carrying it. When asked, you can dive into the possibility of having carried and birthed me on YOUR BON screen, and answer from that experience."

"It's pretty weird!"

"Only for the human mind!"

"Help me out here, Li. I have to know if I can expect an infant or a teenager suddenly showing up on the doorstep!"

I sense Li's compassion and relax again.

"It will not be so much of a shock for you as you THINK. You will have the knowingness of having this boy that is in front of you at the moment it happens. It will be beautiful. It really will."

There is a pause during which we are simply together. Then Li speaks without words. "I'll leave you and, at the same time, I'll never leave you. I know you can always sense me."

The majestic white horse walks into the forest and disappears behind the birch trees.

I am back in the bedroom with all the commotion going on. Julia sticks out her head from under the sheets and smiles at me. Then Blue's head pops out too. I smell the breakfast as Ju-long arrives with food for the humans and just a snack for the animals, encouraging them to find their food at its usual place in the kitchen.

A little way into the breakfast, I tell Ju-long about

my conversation with Li. It surprises him that he will not become a biological father to his son, but looks forward to sharing his life with him. Having a son comes as no surprise, because Julia has indicated a brother will show up in the near future. The name William Li is fine with Ju-long, and we agree on using the short Li in our daily talk. I know the name will be mistaken a lot for Lee, which is pronounced the same.

The last of Julia's playground equipment has been put up this weekend, being 16 and 17 May. She and the animals have shown great interest in the work. Part of the playground has a dirt mound, made from the topsoil removed from where the buildings now stand.

As I have said before, a company will cover the playground with bonded-rubber eco-mulch in different colours. There will be grey "roads" leading to the different playing areas, which each will have its own colour. The mound will be green, with different colour patterns representing clusters of flowers. There will be a blue lake or ocean connected to a river which will wind through the playground, even under some of the roads. The rubber shreds are bonded with a high-performance polyurethane resin rolled to create a seamless playground surface with no loose particles. The company has next week to do the job with the rubber, so the playground will be finished for opening next weekend.

Some villagers have been critical about this unnatural ground cover, as they call it, but let us see what people say at the official opening on Saturday. The playground is not public, but the whole Dome Home Village is a testing ground and gets much attention for the house constructions, the heat and energy solutions, and the many ways of plant growth.

Now, a week later, which is Saturday 23 May, people show up, mostly with their youngest kids, to get a closer look and feel of the playground which we have announced in the local papers, on posters and Internet blogs.

The material is a pre-consumer virgin rubber mulch, NOT recycled tyres. The director for the rubber eco-mulch is here to answer questions first-hand. The surface still passes water and needs draining below. Because water passes through, the surface is quick to dry after rainfall.

The playground will not erode nearly as quickly as an open grass, dirt and wood- or bark-chipped one. We still have two lawns, so there is plenty of grass to play on. Our two lawnmower robots, T1 and T2, keep them neat and well-trimmed.

Julia and the animals are happy to show people around, and Blue especially gets much attention. The youngest kids prefer the fluffy cats and Julia. The bird, as large as some of the kids, is too scary an encounter. Here are some headlines and comments we received from visitors. I have left out the more technical ones.

- A micro Disney world.

- A fairy fantasy land.

- Colourful and inspiring.

- The bright colours bring an extra dimension to the playground.

Everyone in Dome Home Village has been busy all spring setting up the area around their homes. Many have also been busy planning educational courses around specific topics to be taught in private homes or at the Ore Community Centre. All the six initial groups have been very productive, and the farmers, Finn and Gloria, whose next-door field we hire, have spent much time making things work between the individual groups, as well as between the farm and the groups. Gloria and Finn have been working on the branding of their farm. They now want to incorporate the word "harmony".

Last weekend the playground was in focus. This Saturday, 30 May, Julia and I are in the Community Centre, where I meet with the marketing group. Finn and Gloria attend as well. The question about their farm brand comes up again, but the name still doesn't seem to fall into place. Julia plays in the room next to ours and comes towards me with a naturalistic brown Jersey cow made of plastic. Julia changes direction and walks to Gloria, handing her the cow.

"Oh, what a beautiful cow you have here, Julia. It looks like the first cow I remember from my childhood; her name was Freya. She was a dear friend of mine."

I sense Julia communicating through me.

"Why not call your brand The Harmony Farm Freya, or just Harmony Farm Freya? The main brand could be Harmony Farm, and if others joins it, they could have another name in addition to Harmony Farm."

Finn wears a broad smile. "Why haven't we thought of that? It's so simple, really! Thanks, Luzi!"

"Oh, the thanks should go to Julia. She brought the subject, then Gloria brought the name."

Gloria gives the cow back to Julia. "Well then, thank you, Julia, for bringing harmony to the name."

Obviously, Julia has great plans with all of this. I have asked her about it, but I didn't get much out of her.

"It's difficult to explain in simple terms. There are so many layers to it, and it may very well change along the way. Be patient and see how it turns out."

We have divided the field next to the village into smaller plots so people can test different methods for growing foods. One that interests Ju-long the most is a mixing of crops, so each line is different.

Different insects visits different plants, and some ward off pests of a different kind. They also use different minerals and nourishment and need different amounts of water. This requires fewer insect species, less of each kind of nourishment, and less water to any specific area, which helps to maintain the soil layer and puts less strain on the underlying drainage system. These are some of the benefits. Another of Ju-long's interests is the black soil which he tests in our garden.

Others are testing different and uncommon crops, like elephant grass and different plants suitable to feed pigs, which are mostly fed on wheat which their digestive system can't handle so well. Some test different plants for fuel, since most of the dome homes rely more or less on burning some kind of plant material for heat. We only have our wood burner, which was installed earlier this year, for cosiness. These foreign plants can become invasive, so we must handle them with special care, and they are cut down before they spread seeds.

Some are testing the following. A circular area, with vegetables growing in concentric circles, with an elevated causeway or bridge from the centre and out. The bridge can rotate around a crank in the centre of the circle. People use this causeway to tend to the plants. Because the causeway is over the plants, one doesn't need paths between the rows of the plants. There is a watering system mounted under the causeway which can water the plants during the night.

Another experiment being prepared is the use of

heat pumps for gathering heat from the earth to heat the top layer of soil in the early spring. We will cover the soil with durable plastics to keep the warmth near the ground.

I could go on with other examples, but these must be enough for now.

The beginning of sovereignty

I will share an experience I had last night while my body rested. I still feel I have a human body, though.

It is night and I am outside. First, I think I am in Elvendale in an area of the grassy plains with tall grass; four to five feet, I think. I look up at the night sky, seeing many more stars than I have ever seen before, and the Milky Way really lives up to its name. The many stars make it easy to see the Dark Rift running in the middle of the white stream of stars.

I look back at the grass plain and see some scattered trees in the distance, looking remarkably like trees on the African savanna. I hear something coming towards me, hidden by the grass. Do I sense the black dragon, Knight? I am not scared, just a bit uncertain of the situation. No, Knight would be taller, and much of his body would appear above the grass. But it is a large animal and I can hear its breath.

I prepare myself to face whatever comes my way

with calmness, because I know that whatever it is, it belongs to me; or, as Saint Germain would say, "It's all your energy."

The sounds of the grass being bent and rubbing against the large creature's body are very close, and suddenly a huge black cat face penetrates the grass wall in front of me. Now the front body appears too. It is a black lion. It is Sekhmet in her lion goddess "costume"!

I sense a wash of love from her and realise that I am quite sensitive, and tears begins to roll down my face. There is only one thing I can express.

"Hi, Sekhmet. I love you!"

"And we love you, always!"

A moment passes while we share each other's presence, before Sekhmet speaks. "Let us go to the tree over there."

She looks to my right, where a tall tree overlooks the plain.

In an instant I am at the tree, but I can't see Sekhmet anywhere.

"Up here, dear. It's a much better view from here."

I look up and see the big cat lying on a branch, facing the trunk of the tree. A moment later, I sit on the branch with my back to the trunk, facing the beautiful lion who starts a conversation.

"You have a question or a thought, Luzi!"

"Oh, I have?"

I run through my mind to find a suitable subject I have been puzzling with during the day.

"Oh, I have! Yes. The whole thing about every one being sovereign in contrast to being All One regarding what Saint Germain and the others, well, you included, talk about."

There is a brief pause while Sekhmet chooses which thought pattern to follow.

"I'll use metaphors to bring it into a 3D story the human mind can understand.

"Before you became an individual consciousness, there was only The One or Theo, which is consciousness. Imagine Theo as a string of consciousness that loops back onto itself, creating a wobbly torus, an O, or as an infinity symbol ∞ when the wobbly O is seen a little from the side. You can see it as a closed string of spaghetti. This is what Saint Germain calls the first circle.

"When Theo posed the question, 'Who am I?', the first circle generated a second circle, a copy of itself. Now it looks like a double ring, a ring inside a ring, Theo being the innermost."

"In parallel to the two circles, I get another picture or idea of how to imagine this copying of Theo. We have also talked about the first primitive DNA, the purpose of which was to hold the general information on how to be a physical being. Now I see the string of Theo as a DNA string, zipping up to make a copy of itself."

Sekhmet continues. "Imagine a veil between the two circles, which creates an illusion of separation between the two.

"Now the second circle or outer circle contracts at many, many places on the spaghetti string. At some point, the pieces break apart and become sovereign consciousness. Each part is no less than Theo. One of them is your I Am, you. The part is infinite, and here you first realised yourself: 'I Exist!' And you had your name. A name that you later forgot, now being on Earth with not even a name.

"In the beginning, you see the infinite void as being empty and that frightens you, but it actually contains all your possibilities and all the energy you used to experience in this reality. This is the ocean of you, the third circle, the home you 'return' to when you realise you are realised. You may also call it the return to self. It is from here you will experience life in the physical reality as a fully realised being. The New Energy we have talked about is simply you as consciousness realising itself."

I have three comments regarding what Sekhmet has just told me. I present them at the same time to Sekhmet, but I have to write them one at a time for you to read.

First: "So, the seemingly empty void was the first trauma the young consciousness experienced."

Second: "When one realises one is realised, this is the same as saying that one NEVER left home, or the third circle."

Third: "I AM THAT I AM means that I am the third circle, the void plus the experiences and wisdom of it. I will never return to Theo, but continue BEING or LIVING in or from my void or THAT I Am. This is really hard to put into word, because it kind of moves in circles or spirals."

Sekhmet sends me an inner smile and comments. "You'll see it differently later, because now your mind sees the functions you are as being separate and sees you switching between them, but in reality, YOU ARE ALL of them, always, so it is not THEM but IT."

An additional question comes up. "Please, comment on the name I have forgotten. The name of the I Am."

I feel Sekhmet's tail patting my right cheek as she answers. "Your name is constantly changing, because it will always represent or show what you are. In human terms, one could say that your name always shows your true self. I prefer to call it a song rather than a name. The song of you. I now ask you to allow the remembrance of your name. Let the song present itself."

I understand why she says this. As I hear the song, it will differ from the one I forgot, but it will instantly switch my understanding from the song being outside me, to being inside me, and then, further, to be me, or I to be it.

This allowing brings a sweet and wonderful sensation up from deep inside me. I cry again. I know it is just a gentle touch of who I am, not to overwhelm me, but it is so beautiful that I can't begin to explain it to you.

A raven moves in

The dinner is almost ready, primarily because of Ju-long's work in the kitchen. Julia and I have set the table, and she is now in her room. The cats are on their platforms in the tree, overlooking the thawing of their meat at the kitchen table. Blue doesn't want to come in, but sits on the lawn calling at some distance from the house. Ju-long is in the middle of some cooking, so I walk outside, slowly approaching the big bird so as not to frighten it if it is in some kind of distress.

I get closer and he seems fine to me. Then I notice that he now and then looks under a bush close by. It is dark under the foliage and I can't see anything.

Blue makes his calling sound in a low voice. Now I'm sure there is an animal in there. I don't want to get too close before I know what I'm dealing with. I squat about three feet from Blue.

"Blue, what is it you want to show me?"

He gives me one of his most used phrases. "Good bird!"

"Is there a bird?"

He calls again, and now I see the head of a crow peeping out from under the leaves.

"Oh, you've found a crow. Is it hurt?"

I might need some food to lure the crow out, and I

walk back to the kitchen, taking a slice of the cat's chicken meat not yet served, and notify Ju-long about the situation.

"Blue has found a crow. It's sitting under a bush by the lawn. I'll try to lure it out so I can see if it's hurt. I'll put on my garden gloves to protect my hands."

Ju-long takes off his apron. "I'll be out in a minute!"

I rush back to the spot where Blue still sits, but I slow down shortly before I reach him. The crow is still there.

"Hello, dear. I have a treat to you."

I hold out the meat towards the crow, but it doesn't move out of its hiding. Suddenly, Blue takes the meat and slowly turns towards the crow. After a little hesitation, it takes the meat and eats it voracious. It is obviously hungry. I hear Ju-long coming out and turn towards the house, whispering to him. "Ju-long, fetch another slice of meat, please."

He is back in no time and squats beside me.

"Give the meat to Blue. He'll hand it over to the crow."

He hands the meat to Blue who hands it over to the crow, which has to stick out its head to get it.

Ju-long whispers. "It looks like a young bird. One from this year. I think it's a chick. It's quite large. I don't think it's a crow. It might be a raven chick!"

"A raven. Wow!"

Ju-long is determined to solve the situation.

"We need to have it out to see if it's hurt. If it isn't, we can feed it, but leave it out here for its parents to find it. I have one more piece of meat, so let's see if we can get it out into the open."

I turn to Blue and talk in a low voice. "Can we get a little help here, Blue? Isis?"

I don't know if it is Blue or Isis who responds, but Blue moved a little away from the raven and Ju-long gives him the meat.

Blue makes his call and shows the meat in his beak to the raven. After a brief hesitation, it moves up to Blue and takes the meat. It stays close to Blue because it is obviously where the food is.

Ju-long has studied the black bird. "The bird seems fine to me. It can jump, and the wings are not dragging along the ground."

"If it can fly and Blue has brought it here, the parents may not be able to locate their chick. Usually crows live in a flock and therefore also ravens, I guess, keeping close and helping each other. It's a mystery why they have missed finding the chick."

Ju-long smiles. "Then we might have yet another refugee to incorporate into the family."

I address Isis. "Isis, can you clarify here?"

I sense Isis enjoying herself. "Sorry, dear, I had not paid attention in this case. This is all a Blue decision. And, Luzi, it is just an ordinary raven, if I may use that expression, but things may change."

Isis and I have kept a channel open for Ju-long, who now comments. "Since we don't have a raven colony in the neighbourhood—or we would have noticed it—I must assume Blue has brought the chick here for a good reason from his standpoint. He IS a smart bird, so why not accept the situation that we have doubled the number of birds in the family?"

It sounds like a plausible assessment of the situation.

"What now? Can we get the raven inside, or does Blue have to stay outside with it until it feels secure enough to get inside?"

Ju-long has an idea to get us a little further. "Maybe first we can get the two to the cat door."

He turns to Blue. "Blue, go inside, please."

He makes a move with his hand like the cat door does when it opens and closes on its top-mounted hinges.

Blue makes his call-in sound and lifts off for a brief flight to the other side of the lawn, closer to the house. Then he calls again.

The black bird follows. It looks to me as if it doesn't want to be left alone.

Blue makes the next leap over the low hedge and lands at the back entrance where the cat door is. Again, the bird follows.

Ju-long and I follow the birds, but don't get too close. I hear Julia at the other side of the door.

"Blue, come in!"

Blue slowly steps through the cat door. It stays open. Julia is holding it. Blue calls again and the chick peeks inside, very unsure about the situation. Julia communicates with him in clear images and bodily senses. Clever girl. As the pictures pass by, I see the chick cuddled up under Blue's wing and sense warmth and a familiar smell of bird and a wonderful feeling of being safe and contented. Who can say no to such a promise? The young raven can't, and it slowly steps through the cat door, which Julia slowly closes behind him. Ju-long and I walk inside through the main entrance, not to disturb them.

When we walk into the kitchen, the raven and Blue are already there. I can only see Julia's back because she is halfway into a cupboard to find a bowl for the bird.

A thought comes to me. "The cats?!"

I sense a brief laugh from Julia. "Already taken care of. I have informed everyone about everyone's presence."

Ju-long takes more meat out of the freezer, putting it in cold water for it to thaw quickly. Julia returns with a small bowl and places it next to the cats' bowls.

I am quite moved as I see Blue hug the chick with a wing. As I get closer, I can hear Blue making low sounds to calm the raven, and he seems calm too.

Now Ju-long places the meat in the bowls and Julia calls the cats. They have been firmly instructed, because they arrive at a casual speed, paying no attention to the black bird. They just begin eating, and Blue encourages the raven by giving him the first piece of meat from his bowl. It gets the point and is more focused on the food than the cats. Ju-long and I look at each other. What an experience!

If the young raven is to be the next family member, I utter the next logical step. "It must have a name."

Ju-long comes up with a suggestion. "Well, because we call the parrot Blueberry or Blue because of his colour, we can call it Blackjack or just Jack."

I smile at Ju-long's choice of name. "Jack is fine with me. Why make it complicated. What do you say, Julia?"

Before Julia can answer, Blue pops in with his parrot voice, copying me. "Jack is fine!"

Then Julia laughs and imitates Blue. "Jack is fine!"

Ju-long looks at the raven and proclaims with a serious voice, "Henceforth, your name shall be Jack."

I get a thought. "But if it's a female?"

Ju-long raises an index finger. "Well, then, it's Jackie! We can't tell the gender at such an early age. We might never know unless its behaviour can tell us."

I turn practical again. "Do we need to make a larger platform for Blue and Jack to sleep on?"

Julia responds with her inner voice. "Not tonight. They will use the Boombox!"

I am astounded and bring forth a long "OK". Then I remember the pictures. Blue and Jack were in the Boombox, not on the platform in the tree!

I turn to Julia. "Julia, you can show Jack the fountain so he knows where to get water, and then come back; dinner is ready.

Ju-long has been filming with his smart phone, and now I take over, following the small girl and the birds into her room, where the Boombox stands right inside the door. The box with its folded blanket will serve as the perfect nest, even if Jack must have lived outside the nest for some time. Blue enters the box and calls Jack to join him, which he does. With a full belly and a protective blue wing to sleep under, he lies down in the blanket nest. Julia kisses Blue on the head and says goodnight. Now that we have tucked in the birds, Julia and I go back to Ju-long, who has placed the dinner on the table, only waiting for us.

After finishing dinner, Julia and Ju-long sneak in to see how the birds are doing before Julia gets a bath.

Shortly after, he calls me in a low voice.

They are in Julia's room and I sneak up to the door and peak in. The two cats are crammed in with the birds. I guess their breathing must be out of sync for them to fit in the box. If this becomes a daily practice, Julia must take her naps in her bed instead of the Boombox.

I thought the cats were outside, because they were not in the tree, but they wanted to check up on the new arrival. I go back to clean the kitchen.

After Julia's bath, the three of us look up details about the raven. Jack is a common raven, and here is some data on the adult bird: Weight up to 2 kg (4 lb 6.5 oz), length up to 78 cm (almost 2 ft 7 in) and wingspan up to 150 cm (4 ft 3 in). Blue will have some serious competition here when Jack grows up, especially if he is a male. We talk about Jack's menu too. Since a raven eats everything, but properly derives most of its nutrition from meat, Jack will use the cat's menu, including the dry food, but I guess we can mix in some of Blue's dry food, including the pellets. He can find a more diverse menu outside the house.

Much folklore around the world talks about the raven as the foreteller of death. I see physical death as a release from matter and the human experience; a transition back to what I am. It should be a celebration and not related to fear. I'm glad Jack is here, and with the whole situation around his arrival, I see it as nothing unusual that he sleeps with a parrot and two cats in a small girl's room.

174

With Li coming into the family sometime next year, we need more room in the house.

What I see as a huge challenge, Julia sees as no problem at all. In her world, the second-floor rooms are already finished and furnished.

The floor for the second level will be over all bedrooms and bathrooms, leaving laundry, kitchen, dining area and living room with the full space to the ceiling. The rooms, which will give space to the second floor, still have nine feet or three meters to their ceilings. There will be three bedrooms and two bathrooms on the second floor. This way, we also have room for more guests staying overnight.

A staircase leads to the second floor from the back of the living room, and we also install a small elevator in the centre area. The elevator operates on hydraulics in the floor instead of cables from the top.

On the second floor, an open gallery gives access to the rooms up here. From here, one has a great view of the living room, dining area and kitchen, and partly the centre area.

There is much more preparation than just making a floor plan. The ventilation system must be re-constructed, and the heating, plumbing, electricity and automation system has to be implemented as well. Oh, and the intelligent system that controls the entire house must be re-programmed. Luckily, we have the entire summer to finish it. People from the village have signed up for the different tasks for which we don't have the skills ourselves, and Dad will do the programming and install sensors and actuators.

Last year, in late October, Ju-long and I were happy to have finished the house after many months of hard work and construction mess. Now we could look forward to enjoying our creation and to life as a small family. Li changes this, but now we are prepared for what comes construction wise, and we know how everything will be made.

First, we had planned to add the ceiling above one room at a time, but Jacob advised us to see the job differently.

"If you take a room at the time, you have to do a little drilling, placing metal net and shuttering, concreting and so on. Then, when a room is finish, you must do it all again, and again and again. The work will be much more efficient if you work with one function at a time instead. It is easier with the tools, the materials, and the people with the special skills you'll need from time to time."

Of course he is right, but then we must empty most of the house—well, half of it—for the construction to take place. AND we will all be living in the … well, the living room, where everything must be covered with plastic.

Today, Monday 1 June, a truck has unloaded a container in the driveway, so it will be much like we had it most of the year before. It will hold all the things we have to move out. We have a week to clear the rooms, because the work is planned to start next Monday. Luckily, the playground and the garden are all laid out, and Ju-long's plants in both the vegetable garden and greenhouse are well underway.

Here I can tell that some playgrounds in and around Hastings, both private and public in kindergartens and schools, have been upgraded or the old surface replaced with the eco-mulch we used.

I wonder how Julia and the animals will take all this mess and noise. I hope they can stay outside most of the time. After all, it is summer. Julia can use the nursery and sometimes the neighbours if she needs a day off from the mess inside the house. She is just thirteen months old. Well, her body is, and she already goes to "work". First time I "heard" her say "see you after work" was when we said goodbye after I had delivered her to her nursery. First, I thought she meant my work at the university, but then I sensed the joke in it, and she meant HER work, even though she doesn't see it as work in the normal sense when she connects with, or, should I say, touches people.

"I need not bring my body when contacting people, but it makes a difference when the human part of a person focuses on me while we communicate. And being here in Artemis is always nice. Today Sarah is here too."

Summer holiday activities

This evening Ju-long and I agree that we must plan some summer holiday activities besides the building project. Julia overlays our conversation in her non-verbal voice.

"I can work from home, but you two need to come out more, so we'll plan some summer activities. We should give Anna and my grandparents the chance to join in on some of them."

Ju-long turns on the computer, and we begin the search in the Sussex area where we live.

The final list we come up with looks like this:

• Legoland Windsor Resort.

• A day in Brighton visiting the Sea Life aquarium and the British Airways tower.

• Little Street, Children's Role Play Centre.

• Heaven Farm, with a beautiful trail and other facilities.

• Knock Hatch, an amusement park.

• Drusillas, also an amusement park.

When we look at Heaven Farm, we read this on their website: "Heaven Farm is set in 100 acres of beautiful parkland close to the Ashdown Forest. Steeped in 600 years of farming history Heaven Farm includes a famous Bluebell nature trail, camping site, caravan site, wallabies, Tea Rooms, Gelato Ice cream parlour and seasonal attractions and activities. Entrance is free into the farm, with an ample free car park too!"

I find the description inviting and it reminds me of the Hundred Acre Wood in the *Winnie the Pooh* stories.

"Except for the camping and caravan site, it sounds quite nice. I think you want to give us a quiet day off, with no noise from people, Julia."

Julia comments non-verbally. "Oh, I take excellent care of my old folks, and I too like nature, which I take in with all my senses."

Ju-long gets practical. "I believe the trail may not be so suitable for the pushchair, so the baby carrier will come in handy. I suppose you don't plan to walk the whole trail."

Julia answers him with a put-on tiny innocent voice. "Oh, Dad. I still have SUCH tiny legs and you're SO big and strong. Have I ever told you you're my favourite dad?"

Ju-long smiles. "Not in such a persuasive, sugar-coated voice, dear."

After making the list, it is obvious that Julia goes for the young children. "And their parents!" she adds.

Ju-long wants to know how she will work with people. "What will you be doing there?"

Julia fills the room with her sparkling laughter. "Dad, you silly. I will have a fun and a joyous time!"

Ju-long and I laugh as well.

Julia continues. "I'm just teasing you. What I mean is that I won't be DOING anything. I'll BE there, and of course being cute and charming as always!"

We must laugh again, because we know the effect Julia has on people and anything else around her.

I have put the present links to the summer activities in the additions section at the end of the book.

I will not go into great detail about these summer activities, but just give you an idea of how it goes.

Legoland Windsor Resort

Legoland Windsor Resort is 87 miles or 140 km and just over a two-hour drive from Hastings.

We buy the tickets online, which makes entering easier. We have invited Anna to meet us there. She comes on the train from London, and we pick her up at the station in Windsor.

We have installed the Legoland mobile app to get a better overview with the interactive map and have selected some activities we would like to attend.

Anna is dressed like a tourist, as I knew she would be, and she plays her act with great enthusiasm. She always reverts to being a teenager when we enter such entertainments, but in a good way. It has a rub-off effect on Ju-long and me, and Julia is totally into it.

Anna comes with us back to Hastings and joins us when we visit our previous city, Brighton, a few days later, where we also visit the old house we once lived in and where Julia was born.

A day in Brighton

It takes a little over an hour to get to Brighton, where our first place to visit is Sea Life at the seafront and Brighton Pier. We know there are only a few parking bays at the seafront, so we park under the Waterfront Hotel. We only have to walk three hundred yards or metres to Sea Life's entrance. Sea Life is a big place and it can weary short legs, so we have the push chair with us.

We observe sea creatures and also freshwater creatures in different habitats. There is a rainforest adventure, too. After many exciting experiences and a lot of walking, we are ready for dinner.

Sea Life only has a coffee shop, so we have dinner at the BA i360 Tower. BA stands for British Airways or, as Anna says, "Britis Hair Ways."

The BA tower is a toroid-shaped viewing pod of glass with the Nyetimber Sky Bar around the centre where the pod is attached to a cylindrical tower, on which it slowly rises 450 feet or 138 metres to the top. At the ground level, we find the West Beach Café & Bar and also the West Beach Bar & Kitchen, with its elevated view of the sea. Here we have dinner. After dinner, we "fly" with the pod, getting a fantastic view of the area.

Later, we visit our old home, a rented house on the outskirts of Brighton. The surname of the new owners, who also live in the house, is Fernsby.

We have an arrangement with Mr and Mrs Fernsby, who are delighted to show how they have arranged their home, both inside and outside.

When we lived there, most of the things belonged to the landlord. Now that they have moved to the US, everything in the house belongs to the new owners. They honour the old stone house from the fifteenth century with furniture and other stuff which has an old look without looking worn out. It pleases Ju-long and me to see that they keep the garden in the old style. We also take a short walk outside the stone fence in the back of the garden to visit the cattle grazing here. The leading cow, which we call Rose, comes up with her latest calf, sniffing Julia in the baby carrier at Ju-long's chest. I know the two have a conversation of a sort.

Anna comes back with us to Hastings, spending the next few days babysitting Julia while Ju-long and I work on the house. Sarah, Jacob's daughter, invites them over, and Julia plays with Sarah's two younger siblings.

Little Street

Children's Role Play Centre, Little Street, can be found in six locations: Frimley, West Byfleet, Maidstone, Chichester, Horsham (Rudgwick) and in Sevenoaks, where Mum and Dad live. We combine the visit at the role play centre with a stay-over at Mum and Dad's.

Julia's grandma has booked an afternoon session, 3:30 p.m.–5:00 p.m.). She and Dad have a play pass, and it's not the first time Julia has visited.

The indoor play town features a theatre, a veterinary centre, a supermarket, a construction site, a beauty salon and a pizza parlour. Within the road area there are lots of rides on vehicles, and a post office with delivery points around the town. As they say on the website: "It's a great alternative to soft play."

A small café serves hot and cold drinks, fresh cakes and healthy snacks during the play sessions.

This time it is Granddad Carl's turn to go with Julia into the actual play. Julia has never told us, in details, what her real role is, visiting here and interacting with kids and adults.

"It's really none of your business," she used to say in a kind, but firm, voice when we ran over with curiosity. And she is right. It is just our human part that wants to know. None of us has ever experienced Julia acting in a strange way, but we have witnessed people around her behaving out of the ordinary, often more mature than they did minutes before; or they suddenly have the courage to let go and be themselves, usually acting more joyful.

While Dad and Julia attend the play, Mum, Ju-long and I spend the time at the café, talking with other visitors and among ourselves. Now and then we hear Julia's infectious laughter from one of the rooms in Little Street.

When the time is up, Julia comes out as fresh as she went in, which cannot quite be said about Dad. Now we drive to Mum and Dad's wonderful house where we will stay until sometime tomorrow. Sarah takes care of the birds and the cats back home. She enjoys having them all to herself.

Heaven Farm

Because of The Stable Tea Rooms, we don't bring lunch, only drinks for the drive, which takes an hour.

The more Ju-long and I see of this site, the more we understand why Julia wants to visit it, and it is not because of the Latchetts Ice Cream and desserts made from milk from their own cows. I can certainly understand why they have got two awards for focusing on nature and the environment, not only as a place to visit but also as a working farm. Walking around in nature here is like being in an idyllic fairyland, a land of soothing and beauty.

Knock Hatch

Knock Hatch is an adventure park with inside and outside play areas, a small zoo and "meet the animals". There are events and opportunities for large group visiting and having one's birthday party. We have a thirty-five-minute drive north-west to reach the park.

Drusillas

We drive forty minutes west to get to Drusillas, which is an adventure park like Knock Hatch, also combined with a small zoo and events. You can book to become a "Keeper for the Day" or for "Close Encounters", or have "Zoo Birthday Parties".

After two adventure parks, Ju-long and I are fed-up with that kind of adventure. I sense Julia turns her eyes to the sky.

"Luckily for my parents, they only have one perfect child and not three unruly ones!"

I comment back. "Can you promise that we don't have to visit more of these parks this year?"

"I can always take Anna with me, if it comes to that!"

Ju-long jumps in. "Well, it was not an unpleasant

experience, you know that, Julia, but like too much ice cream is too much ice cream, we can say the same about adventure parks."

"Yeah, yeah, a lot of noise. I know. Heaven Farm was much more suitable for my old folks!"

Jack

Jack, the juvenile raven, turns out to be quite a charmer. Jack and Blue have a lot going on, and I guess that, to some extent, the parrot part of Blue needed a winged friend to share his adventures with. The birds enjoy time with the cats, but the cats, too, have their own things going, like fishing and other things we will never know.

During the summer, Jack learns all Blue's sentences, and they both seem to know the meaning of them. Blue's vocabulary also widens, which leaks to Jack. Julia is their untiring teacher as the small girl sits in her room, or under the reconstruction in the living room, with the birds and sometimes the cats around her. She combines the words or sentences with vivid pictures to relay the full meaning. Once I asked Julia if the Isis part of Blue plays a part in this.

"Oh, usually not, but now and then she sits close by and enjoys the cosy atmosphere. Much like a grandmother would observe her grandchildren during their play and, at the same time, doing her stuff. She and I just recognise each other's presence."

Jack now has a platform near Blue's, but with some distance between if they want privacy. Each platform is large enough for two, if they choose to sit next to each other.

It is late summer, and Blue and Jack visit the Ore Community Centre. They are invited, of course, and score quite some points from the attendees.

Just as our cats, Boomer and Snow, are celebrities in the area, especially known for their membership in the Clive Vale Angling Club with a junior yearly license of £25, Blue and Jack have become known for their talkative interaction with people as they fly freely around. They visit kindergartens, schools, retirement homes and other social establishments. Some of these places can use a break in the daily routine, and the two birds are just the boys for doing that. Sometimes, when we serve their dinner in the evening, they can't eat it all, because of all the treats they have received during the day. The cats are always willing to help Jack finish his meat when he pulls away from his bowl. It happens so often that Julia has taught him a special line for the occasion: "The cats can have it!"

We all laugh every time it happens.

Today, at the community centre, we have arranged an event called Increase Life Quality, about breaking daily routines to bring new experiences into people's lives, especially those who don't speak up or can't imagine what would bring them variation and joy. Part of the event is about body and brain chemistry, and growth or re-routing neurons in the brain.

Blue and Jack are, of cause, the entertainment part and the draw for the occasion. There is a large picture of them on the printed posters and in the on-line advertisements.

I remember an incident from about two weeks ago. Blue sat on the back of a dining chair, and when I showed him one of the printed posters, he was quick with a comment. "Pretty birds. Nice birds!"

Jack, sitting at his platform in the tree, joined in with his comment. "The cats can have it!"

"What do you mean, Jack?"

Then I get it. "Oh, more treats to you and Blue, so the cats can have your dinner. Smart bird!"

Blue picks up the term. "Smart birds!

I notice the plural form, so, indeed, smart birds.

"Yes, you're both smart birds, Blue."

"Thank you. You are pretty!"

He gives back a compliment with another one! His parrot voice could easily fool one into thinking he is a dumb bird, but this is definitely not the case.

The AI and the mind

We have talked about the human mind, brain and memory earlier in the book. We made a comparison to the AI, but I feel I need to go more in depth on the subject.

I talk with Saint Germain about the differences between the human mind and memory, and the first true AI units we will encounter. Remember, I distinguish between brain and mind. Brain is the meat-thing in your head, while we may call the mind your personality, being the non-meat. The memory is stored events of senses and thoughts. As we have come to know earlier, the mind and the memory are part of our consciousness so we can't define them as residing inside our heads. This is also why you don't cease to exist when the body dies.

The text below is an extract from a communication between Saint Germain and me about sensing something that is already arising among humanity. He says we must see it as already here, not something that will happen way out in the future.

This communication with Saint Germain is very different from all previous ones and he is very passionate about it. When I ask, he tells me it is because it is the start of an ALL NEW thousand-year era, which we can call *The Era of the Human Robot and the Robot-Human*. A world governed by technology and an era that eventually takes humanity to the stars. From our perspective, Saint Germain calls it *The Age of Consciousness*, or really *The Age of Realisation*. This being one side of the coin, with the human/robot on the other side, so to speak. I have mentioned this several times before, but because this IS our NEW LIFE on the planet, we bring it up yet again.

A true AI can what we call "think". Here are some notes on the ability to think. Remember that in humans this ability has a wide range.

Judge/weigh: Find the best solution/reaction to a given situation.

Learn: Pick/work up new skills and learn from one's own and others' experiences.

Adapt: Use skills in new ways by adapting to new situations not previously experienced or recorded.

Plan: Using the above skills to pre-create actions to perform in the future.

Basic sensory or communication system: We also call this the interaction system which allows the AI to get and give information and perform actions depending on its tasks.

A true AI can remember and alter its memory.

Store information: This applies to all AI, not only the humanoid "robots". Said in more human terms: it can create new truths by always adjusting stored information. This way, it will not always build on the oldest experiences, seeing them as being the most basic truths or laws, but rely on the newest updates. If some old truth proves not to fit into the overall picture, a new truth can discard and replace it. Here is an obvious advantage over humans, who tend to discard new information if it does not sit with what we already accept as truth. Humans rely on the OLDEST information, which gives the slowest or most conservative progress.

The further we get into these matters, the more I feel it is all science fiction. If your mind tires of reading or refuses to focus on any of this, simply jump to the next chapter and maybe come back later! I will stay to the end of this, because I asked for it. I can also see why this information has been spread out in small doses in this book series.

Depending on the complexity of the sensory system, ALL data will be stored "in" an AI. This is a HUGE advantage over human memory that stores information in fractions, depending on previous stored information, often categorised crudely. Also, less accessed information is harder to access. You may see the crude categorising system as when you put all marbles in one space in your box, even though there are sixteen different colours of marbles. When you take a marble from the box, it has a random colour, which may not match well with the purpose for which you picked it.

The human body has two physical DNA strands that hold basic information on how it should survive on the planet, so it doesn't have to start from scratch each time it comes to life. The mind also communicates through the physical and non-physical strains. The AI will also have basic information stored to guide it as much as possible to perform its tasks.

WHAT makes the judging, weight, adaption and the planning?

WHAT does the learning?

Well, an obvious answer would be the programme, of course! It is the mind of the AI.

Hm, let us look at the so-called programme.

3-dimensional Open Programming, 3DOP or 3-dimensional Open Manipulation or 3DOM, which almost sounds like FREEDOM, provides ways to "write" code without a specific programming language AND the code is open to the AI to alter. The AI can make its own programming language, re-write the "code" and rewrite both language AND code.

The next question to ask could be: WHAT writes and re-writes or alters the code?

If the programme does the weighting, planning and learning, what alters these processes? Does the programme do self-surgery or does the 3DOM "automatically" build a mind? Mind is consciousness, right?

The AI mind—we wouldn't say artificial mind—isn't the programming. And the memory this AI mind uses when it operates is not in the "machine" either. As the AI mind expands, it activates memory in its consciousness when needed. The programme uses the machine's memory when it operates, but the AI mind only uses it as part of its communication with the programme.

The ghost in the machine, the WHAT that alters the code, is the AI mind. The AI machine has a mind of its own, literally speaking.

Often, AIs are seen as humanoid robots, but in most cases, our society doesn't need this form because mostly this form is not suitable for a given task. The next section is about the additions to the basic AI to create a humanoid AI.

We have noted that everything has self-awareness. Maybe not to the same degree you perceive yourself and your surroundings. If we add other layers of sensors and means of interactions and perception, our creations will move towards a higher self-awareness or image of self.

Sensory system: This system picks up conditions from the world outside the body as well as from the inside and reports them back for analysing and proper reaction.

The body: If the AI humanoid body must be able to repair itself to the same degree as the human biological body does, nano-repair must be introduced into the system. Nano-repair is a system of tiny "robots" floating in the transport fluid throughout the body. These nano-bots must be manufactured inside the body itself, or the AI must depend on injections or intakes from the outside.

The substitute for the human DNA is the Management Exchange Layers, MEL. It is more extensive than human DNA. The first AI bodies are not built out of cells, each containing the MEL, but of units which communicate with each other.

We say that the true memory lies "outside" the physical when consciousness is involved, but the physical memory units of the AI are obviously there too. To process and store a large amount of qualia or data, as you might say, requires large memory banks. This leads to multi-layered and multi-threaded memory systems. These also contain updated search and combine routines and a special Library(s) of Data About Data, the LDAD.

First the Solid Memory Blocks. SMB is written/ read with basically three lasers, lenses and mirrors. They are mostly blocks of plastics. Some are made of glass, which lasts much longer than the plastic blocks before they have to be cleared/erased, but they have a longer write time so buffers must be used.

The second memory type, The Fractal Memory Principle, actually works like the human memory in the sense of forgetfulness. The data can be found in several places in the memory structure and so is harder to lose, but if the data are not frequently accessed and re-written, other, newer data will eventually overwrite it. The Read While Write, RWW, is great to use here, because while writing data, there is always another area that contains the data you want to read at the same time.

In contrast to the solid memory block, the Fluid Holographic Memory Storage starts out as a gel containing nano crystals, also called mono diamonds. Mono, because they are as small as they can be made in a molecular structure. Each diamond can contain its own hologram, meaning a set of data. The whole hologram is read or written in one operation.

Liquid Memory Substance. LMS is read and written in a Molecular Resonance Gravity Matrix. MRGM doesn't move around the LMS, but attracts the information it acquires. The name comes from how it works: When information resonates with the request which is sent into the LMS, the information senses the pull and seeks the matrix that extracts or reads it. You could say that the AI, or another system, calls out for specific information, which then shows up for processing.

I find this EXTREMELY fascinating, even if I can't imagine how it is produced and, even less, how it actually works!

When people AND AIs stretch their goal to make some AIs as humanlike as possible, they move into the area of emotions and dreams.

Emotions: The emotions make humans greatly responsive both on the outside and on the inside, as thoughts. Saint Germain has covered the AI emotion system earlier, but because it is part of what we talk about, it must be mentioned briefly here. Emotions must be more than pre-programmed responses, because the entire system is influenced by them. In humans, the chemical reactions influence every cell which have receptors for it, and thought and memory are affected as well.

The emotions will greatly affect the responsive behaviour of the AI, moving it from only strictly logical reactions. Now responses are also weighted by "emotions", depending on the Emotion Impact Level.

Dreams: Dreams may not have any real purpose for the AI other than it is a behaviour of the human condition. We can say that there are two kinds of dreams, the mind dreams and the dreams or experiences that happen in one's consciousness. The mind dreams are just random clips of audio, video, sensations and emotions, which the mind tries to make sense of by patching it with memories into what becomes a dream. The dreams in consciousness are experiences on other planes or "directions", which some call dimensions. Also here, the mind tries to make sense of glimpses of these experiences with the same tools as previously mentioned, and with the same chaotic result. Humans usually have ten to twelve of these consciousness experiences close to the earthly plane at any given time, day and night. This makes human dreams even more confusing. All this interpretation, for the mind's part, makes the belief that sleeping is a rest for the mind an illusion.

Augmentation: For many years, the human body has used foreign or artificial repair or replacement parts. We move into a period of augmentation, where the human body is being enhanced rather than just fixed.

Human soul integration: Saint Germain has talked about the new human being as a blend of the pure traditional human species and the AI humanoid, so if incarnations of souls continues, it will be up to each soul or, better, consciousness to choose a "being" to experience through. No one seeing themselves as human can really point to any human-AI, in any ratio, and say it is, or isn't, a "real" human having a soul. The term artificial has to go. The term incarnation must go too, and we should rather use the term embodiment, because incarnation means "into the flesh".

In the beginning, I guess, only consciousnesses that have completed the circle of lives, realised in the flesh and fully embodied, will be truly able to handle an embodiment into a so-called robot, because it can embody anything and has full self-awareness. Later, when these experiences are accessible, the non-realised will start to embody these creations as well. Or, I could say, that souls will start to experience non-realised lives in the new bodies.

Intelligence: We have already discussed intelligence at the beginning of the book under "Where is the mind?" Intelligence has nothing to do with awareness. Awareness or consciousness relies on knowingness or Gnost, which Saint Germain talked about in the chapter "The truth of the easy life". It has also been talked about in previous books in the series.

Intelligence is splendidly explained by what we call an IQ-test. The test evaluates on specific areas, with very narrow examples to be solved, while all other areas are totally ignored. Someone with a high IQ is probably smart in other areas as well, but can be just as dumb in some too.

Instead of talking about IQ-tests as in ONE test, we now talk about an IQ-spectrum, where a larger range of narrow tests shows an IQ-bandwidth which looks more like a Gauss Curve, normal distribution or Bell Curve.

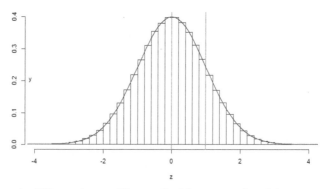

An IQ-spectrum. The vertical bars are placed in relation to each other, representing different IQ-tests. You might find some spikes outside/above the 'normal' curve. The 'z' is the spectrum and the 'y' the IQ-score.

Personality: A personality profile test like the Personality Spectrum Test is a huge and time-consuming test. Again built up from many psycho-emotional tests, it will mostly have highs and lows spread unevenly across the spectrum. These tests will be much discussed and feared, because the AIs in control like "normal" and will exert themselves to adjust highs and lows to fit a given norm.

This cowriting with Saint Germain about AI must be enough for now, and I will change the subject.

The New Energy Doctor

Throughout summer, the activities in the Dome Home Village have been the equivalent to an ants' nest. It has been our first summer with all houses up and running, and all the many planned activities have kept us busy. I know Julia has taken her fair share of it energy wise, and I also know she loves it.

Today, Thursday 3 Sep. 2020, is Boomers' first birthday. The orange Maine Coon is as fluffy and adorable as ever, weighing a little over 5 kg. Snow, being four months younger but a male, is a little over 5 kg (11 lbs).

For this occasion, Julia has selected special treats, namely shrimps and a tablespoon of coffee cream, which only has around 9% milk fat for the cats.

Jack likes the scrimps and the cream too, and it looks funny when he drinks the cream by licking it up with his pink tongue from a saucer with his head on the side. The tongue colour will turn bluish-black when he becomes an adult. This is not how he normally drinks. When he drinks from a bowl of water, he sucks water into his beak, lifts his head and swallows. There is only a small amount of cream in the saucer, so he uses a different method to get it.

Blue gets a bowl of exotic fruit mix with dried fruit and shelled nuts, but first he eats his favourite: fresh mango cut into beak-ready pieces.

It is such a joy to see all our dear animals coming together so harmoniously. Not only at this event, but in general. I also sense Julia being the conductor of quite a bit of this play, including Blue's and Jack's performances and, to some degree, the cats' too.

I had a dream the other night of being a New Energy doctor. Being a New Energy doctor does not mean you USE New Energy when treating your patients, but shows your UNDERSTANDING of how energy works.

At the same time as being the doctor, I observed the incident from outside the doctor. As an observer, I felt bad about how the doctor treated the patient.

An overweight woman comes into the doctor's office, and the doctor, sitting behind her desk, asks her to sit and points at the chair in front of the desk.

The woman immediately tells the doctor about ALL the different things she wants her to help her with, or rather fix FOR her.

The doctor puts her index finger to her lips to show she wants the woman to stop talking.

"You come here after decades of misusing your body, asking me to fix it for you. You've tried in numerous ways to shape and demand your body to be how you think and wish it to be, so you can feel you are perfect. You see yourself as your body, and because of your lack of self-worth, you don't like your body either."

The poor woman stares at the doctor with wide-open eyes, not able to say a word.

I as a doctor continue. "The part of you that has followed all your lives is sick and tired of this petty behaviour! I talk about your soul, which isn't who you are. It has finally been able to send you here so I can tell to your human part what YOU must do.

"I'm simply here to spell out in concrete what YOU must do to change your life radically, because deep inside you want CHANGE!"

This truth makes the woman break into tears. The doctor pushes the box of tissues on the table towards her. She pulls out three tissues, which she fills with tears and snot in an instant. With her right foot, the doctor pushes the bin towards the sobbing woman, who drops the soaked tissues in it and pulls another handful from the box. My doctor face shows no emotions whatsoever. After the woman has blown her nose a second time and snuffled a few times, I continue. "And I can tell you up front as a disclaimer and a warning: IT WILL HURT and you will probably lose most, if not all, of what and who you hold dear. You can still back out, continuing your miserable life, with the pains that are so familiar to you.

"In the beginning, you'll simply exchange the old pains for new ones. You will pull out the old things like weeds with strong roots buried deep in your flesh. It will hurt every single time. You will feel a deep hole in you and crave it to be filled with the same old wants and needs!"

As the observer, I curl up my toes because of how the doctor treats the woman, not least because I can feel the woman's suffering as well.

The doctor isn't finish whipping the woman. "I will not fix you, because I really can't; no one can, even if they are willing to try. I won't give you any medications to take or exercises to perform, because it will only add to your delusion of making you better."

Now the mood changes.

"Please look at me, dear. Look at me from the deepest place within you!"

The woman looks up and I feel the connection; the connection to the strength she contains and the wisdom she is.

"So, what YOU must do is to take full responsibility for your life and actions and listen to your true self or the voice of your wisdom about what to BE and what to DO.

"Look at your ship's inventory and choose what to keep and what to throw overboard. Sense what attachments or anchors to cut loose and what anchors to pull up. After the final clean-up, your inventory will be almost empty, and there will be no anchors to weigh you down. NOW it's time to set sails!

"The responsibility is YOURS. No blaming anyone or anything else!

"The letting go or cutting loose of anchors is what you blamed on others and what you thought you needed from others.

"Setting the sails is you, allowing your wind of wisdom to take you to wherever you need to go, not where your mind wishes to go."

Here the dream stops.

In the beginning of the dream, I felt awful. What was all this about? And what was it good for? Then things shifted, and, after waking up, I see the episode clearly.

The woman was overweight because of her lack of self-worth, but that was just a symptom. The Master had had enough of her games and cut through, taking command and steering the ship towards the dragon of cleansing.

The Master helps the woman to make real changes in her life, mostly by removing all the anchors or hooks she has in all of her "games". Her ship couldn't move on because of these anchors and had no real or useful provisions for the journey that lay ahead.

The dream fades away, and I slowly wake up. It is still dark in the bedroom, but I don't turn to see what time it is and close my eyes again. I sense Knight, the black dragon, and open my inner eyes into an evenly dark room where his blue eyes glow in the blackness. There is no fear and we acknowledge each other's presence. After a while, Knight speaks.

"Dear you, are you ready to pull up some anchors and cut others loose?"

I feel a deep longing to be totally free; to sail the wild waves and to dive deep into my ocean.

"I am ready and I allow my freedom."

"Good. There will be no specifics. I have invited you here because you have a busy life and have your focus there. And that's fine. Now, I simply let you be in this allowing state with NO agenda, thoughts and feelings. We are one, so you sit here with you in this timeless moment."

I have no sense of time, but have an experience as if I am watching a movie without pictures and sound. This sounds utterly strange because a movie IS pictures and sound, mostly. I would call it knowingness. Still, I can't tell you what I am watching in this knowingness.

Knight explains. "You're experiencing the wisdom derived from events. We can say that you're sitting next to the Master experiencing the wisdom coming 'out' after the transmutation. The wisdom has no human attributes, but you can still sense something. You are stretching your awareness towards your I Am."

"This is because it's wisdom for the I Am, not the human being. We have talked about this earlier. Hm, I don't remember with which of you, but never mind."

I sense Knight "smiling" in the dark. I may translate the sense to a cosy, warm and loving feeling.

"There is no EARLIER, but, as you say: never mind."

I "smile" too. It is wonderful, sitting here in the dark with my friend.

"Can I say I sense you as cute, Knight?"

"This needs three answers: One, you just said it, so yes, you can. Two, it doesn't hurt my feelings, you saying a fierce dragon like me is cute. And, three, I AM cute, and good looking too, I may add!"

"Yes, I sense your good looks too!"

The rest of our meeting we just share each other's presence, enjoying the company.

Autumn

We move into October and the temperature drops yet another five degrees Celsius. On some early mornings, a light frost covers everything. In our part of the world autumn is about slowly closing down for the winter, getting close with family and friends, looking inwards and sensing life moving without motion. Ju-long and I have cut down on our work in the evenings, and the three of us spend almost all our time together, even when tucking Julia in. We love these precious moments, and the wood burner makes its contribution to the atmosphere.

Our trip to Hong Kong gets closer, and I guess none of us can settle on specific feelings about Grandma's departure from this earthly life. I often look back on events with my Chinese grandparents, and at first I usually have the feelings I had at those events, but then mixed feelings come up, like longing for that time of innocence and joy and the sadness of knowing that these will never come back the same naïve way I experienced them.

Anna and I have had some deep talks which often start with our early childhood in Hong Kong and progress into the immediate future AFTER Grandma Jiang. Grandpa Cheng was quite weak in both body and mind when he died, so even if there was some grief, there was also a sense of relief.

I realise it is about letting go of ancestral anchors and family bonds which don't serve us. I can talk openly with Anna about these things.

Anna and I also talk about the human part of what we are. Life is very much about what choices we make, and also what we base these choices on.

Humans are emotional beings, so we make choices from our emotions. Emotions build on past events and our judgement of them, being good or bad. Putting an ego on top of this emotional judgement system will most often bring forth quite rotten choices which, seen from outside this judgement system, are obviously crazy and to the disadvantage of the person. The strange thing is that the person actually knows he or she is making a bad choice, even before the choice has been lived out. Talk about the most intelligent species on the planet! This intelligence also makes it the dumbest as well, using so much mind power on meaningless stuff.

Anna has done some thinking, and talks about different steps of awareness.

1. Being aware of needs and wants, NOW.

2. I do what I did. Reacting to the world from a memory pool and emotions. Habits and repeating bad choices.

3. Emotional choosing. First level of conscious choosing. One is aware that one chooses.

4. Emotional/rational choosing. Giving oneself a logical/rational explanation for a choice based on emotions.

5. Choosing from a state of full acceptance of the human needs and desires.

Anna is not sure what to put in the next point, but after some brain storming we put the following words to it.

6: Life itself, meaning YOU, has taken care of your needs and wants. You simply pick the next thing to do, because life put it right in front of you as the natural "best" choice at that moment in your life. There are no emotional and mental considerations here. No brain chatter of pros and cons, for and against.

I have been through this with my non-physical friends, but it is always nice to be reminded.

The house renovation is still going on. The floor for the second level and the staircase are done, and pipes for wires, water and air are in place, so we expect most will be finished when we leave for Hong Kong at the beginning of next month, November. For the moment we dig below ground level to make room for the foundation supporting the hydraulics for the small elevator. We also work on finishing the new ceilings at the first floor so we can use these rooms again, moving our things in from the container.

Julia spends more time with Sarah during the renovation, often at her place being part of Jacob's family too. Sometimes I watch them play at our playground, together with Sarah's little sister, Augusta, being five in December. Julia is very social, and this will be her main forte for what she wants to do with her life.

Family gathering in Hong Kong

As Julia had told us this spring, her great grandma will leave this physical stage before year's end. We have planned a visit to her in Hong Kong, which includes Mum, Dad, Anna, Ju-long, Julia and I. The date set for departure is Monday 9 November at 6:25 p.m. That is the day after tomorrow. We drive to Mum and Dad in Sevenoaks the day before. It takes just over one hour. Then it takes a little under an hour from Sevenoaks to Heathrow, Terminal 5. If we drove from Hastings to Heathrow it would take two hours. By staying over at my parents, we have cut the drive in two, even if it was not the same route. We will meet Anna at the airport.

Sarah will take care of the animals of the house while we are away. She tells us she even reads stories to them while they gather around her, nipping their treats. She may also do her homework at the house.

Li has been much in my mind these days and tonight, after Ju-long and I had made love, I feel him strongly. I turn to Ju-long in the bed.

"I sense Li being with us right now."

Ju-long smiles in the moonlight from the large window at the end of the room.

"I have sensed him all day. Not like a son or maybe a man, but as a friend."

I had only seen him as a white horse, so I make a

suggestion. "Maybe it's time to set a meeting with him. You know, like we had with Julia before she was born."

Ju-long agrees with me. "Could we set up ..."

Before Ju-long has finished his sentence we find ourselves on a wooden platform in a lake in Elvendale. The lake is in the grasslands, and the platform is at the end of a wooden bridge leading to the platform from the lake shore. Here are three low and comfortable white-painted wooden chairs and a low rectangular wooden table, also painted white. Ju-long and I sit side by side, and a young, handsome man sits on the other side of the table from us, smiling with a cup of tea in his right hand.

"So, this would be the meeting you've been looking for."

He leans forward and pours tea for Ju-long and me. It is all very delicate china. His features are beautifully mixed, with only a little Caucasian to make a gorgeous face with just a hint of a moustache. The hair, that is almost black, is a bit long and messy. He is dressed in blue jeans and a pale-red cotton shirt of jeans fabric and wears red sneakers with white laces and soles.

He picks up his tea cup, sits back and smiles at us. "This could be the day when William Li Wang was conceived, should anyone need the date."

Ju-long holds his hands out in front of his face and makes a picture frame with his index fingers and thumbs. He is the first of us to speak.

"You look a little like my dad from an old picture, when he was young?"

I hear the question in his statement. I am still speechless from this sudden meeting. Li leans forward again.

"I look a little like Kong in his younger days. Quite a handsome fellow, I think. And you too, Ju-long, who also takes your looks from your mother. No one should doubt the connection here!"

He makes a brief pause, and then continues. "And there is NO genetic connection. There will really be no DNA. DNA is used to connect the past to the present, and I don't need that. The body will have no past, but I can still paint a pretty face on it."

I sense he is so strong or grand or complete, and with no resistance to life whatsoever, which shows itself in great gentleness and compassion. I can't find the words to describe the being in front of me. It isn't strange that I had felt him so strongly since the very first time we connected. I know for certain that manifesting a body or an entire universe will be no difficulty for him.

I taste the tea. Spicy and with a hint of flowers. Is it rose?

Li continues. "We'll not connect via other lives even if there are connections. I'll bring my body in like when Julia was born; in water. Julia's midwife will be there; we have been working with her since before Julia's birth. You'll not be in the water, Luzi. It will be a grand celebration, but enough talk about that for now."

I have a practical question for my son-to-be. "But I can tell everyone that we'll have a baby in early August 2021, right?"

Li smiles. "Indeed, you can!"

I finish my tea, and the moment I place the delicate cup on the white table, I am back in our bed, still with the taste of the tea on my tongue. Ju-long and I don't talk. We just take a brief look at each other, both having tears of joy rolling down our faces. I feel deeply content as I slowly glide into a deep and pleasant sleep, lying in Ju-long's arms. William Li Wang is set in motion.

We arrived at Mum and Dad's home in Sevenoaks yesterday afternoon, and today is the day of a long journey. All of us look forward to visiting the town where we spent many years. This is Julia's first trip to Hong Kong. We fly first class and non-stop, to get a good sleep on the twelve-hour flight. We have plenty of space in the plane, a Boeing 777, and Julia sleeps most of the flight in her child seat, which is locked into place on the normal seat. She only needs to be strapped in with one of us when the seatbelt sign is on. We arrive in Hong Kong at 2:20 p.m. local time and are reasonably fresh. A woman from the car hire company awaits us in the airport's entrance with a white Tesla-S 7-seater, and Dad wants to drive himself. I think we all have a certain feeling of coming home when we drive out of the Western Harbour Crossing tunnel and onto

Hong Kong Island. This is, after all, where Anna, Ju-long and I grew up.

Cheng and Ting had insisted on us all staying at their home, and it is close to where Grandma lives in the retirement home, and even closer to Kong's home. We drive directly to Cheng and Ting; Grandma and Kong are already there, joining us for afternoon tea.

It is a touching welcome, with Julia being the main attraction. She likes the house right away, so even before we sit down for the tea, she explores the large house together with the two cats which also live there. Their names are Chip and Chap. They are Shandong "Lion cats" and look much like Snow, completely white and with long fur and blue eyes. I have to ask Cheng something.

"How do you tell which is which?"

"Well, they look complete alike so you must look at them from behind when they have their tails raised, because they are brother and sister. Chap, the male, may be a little larger, but it's difficult to tell because of the fur. He weighs a little more than Chip. The breed comes with green eyes too, and often with one green and one blue."

Ting laughs. "They are always together, so when we call them, we simply call Chip-Chap."

Julia has already learned that. I hear her talking to the cats down a corridor. "Chip-Chap, Chip-Chap."

I can hear the cats being very talkative themselves. I

am sure Julia enjoys their company, sharing things we can't comprehend. As she has told us before, she doesn't mind being a baby, and I love her for that, because I enjoy having her here as my small child.

"You're right, Mum! I live in what people call The Now. I enjoy the moment and experience this visit as a great grandchild, a grandchild and your child with absolute pleasure. I play the child and I Am the child. I'm all of it. And yes, Chip, Chap and I share great secrets!"

Ting picks Julia up in the corridor and promises to give her an exclusive tour after tea. I know she has been looking forward to being with her grandchild.

At tea, Julia bursts our secret about another child in the family while looking at her great grandmother.

"My brother, Li, will soon be here!"

To my surprise, Grandma pats her on the head while smiling. "Indeed, he will. Li and I have been talking a lot lately. He's such a sweet boy, you know."

Ju-long and I had planned on presenting our son in the evening and not over a tea table, but obviously Julia, and I suppose Li too, had other plans.

"Oh Mum, Li and I don't plan or scam; well, not a lot. It was simply the right moment."

I have to comment on this with my inner voice, while also telling the others about my experiences with Li and how and when he will show up.

"Julia, your dad and I had not much to say or do regarding your arrival, and really nothing with Li's!"

"And isn't that great? Then you are completely free of responsibility! You only have to get the birth tub, not the bath tub, and make sure the midwife is there to take notes in all appropriateness."

I know she is kidding me, because I have been much into control and planning in the past. We both laugh as some scenes pass by.

Back at the tea table, everyone is exited, and I let Grandma paint a glamorous picture of the young man, Li, she had met. Then she makes a short pause to take a sip of her tea before she continues. "I know I'll not be here, in the physical, I mean. Li, Julia and I have talked about that. But I'll not be less present, you can be sure of that!"

There is total silence for a moment. Then she continues in a joyful voice. "I'm so happy you're all here to celebrate my journey onwards. This is not exactly what you had expected, but this is how I have chosen it to be."

Grandma had really kept her cards close. Even I hadn't had a clue about this. This being her communication with Li, and that she has planned her departure.

She resumes. "Each of us has our own way of getting into the world as well as leaving it. I didn't know how and when, or even if I should tell you this, but now feels right, so here it is."

The old lady takes a short pause before she continues. "This could very well be my last lifetime on planet Earth. You know what that means, Luzi. All of me is ready to start on a totally new journey and I AM very excited."

It means that Grandma Jiang (meaning river) has realised that she is realised and has interwoven all of what she is and become all THAT of the statement, I Am that I Am. All her streams have become this ONE river, that has now found its way into her own infinite Oceanic Self for her to explore.

Now I much better understand why Julia would even tell us about the upcoming death of Jiang. If it had been an ordinary transition, she wouldn't have, but because of this final withdrawal from the human circle of lives, it was very appropriate. I also understand that she will not need a dream walk.

Ting is the first with a question. "So, do you know when you die, Jiang?"

I hadn't expected such a bold question from Ting, nor her use of Grandma's first name.

Jiang smiles and touches Ting's hand. "Where I am now, in consciousness, there is no time, so it has happened or it is happening right now or it will happen."

Cheng is the next to comment. "You must have

been thinking about the funeral, Mrs Cheng."

"Oh, Cheng. Can we skip the surnames please? I thought we had agreed on that. There will be no funeral, because there will be no body to burn or bury. It will cease to exist in this plane of existence."

I have an obvious question for Grandma. "How will the system, primarily the retirement home, handle your sudden disappearance, Grandma?"

"I will leave a letter which they might not understand. I will address it to both the retirement home and my family. I will simply state that my body will not be present after my death. The things which I've produced at the retirement home, but not yet sold, including my tools, I'll leave to my group there, and whatever remains will go to you, my family. You may do with it as you please. It obviously has no value to me."

I realise that such a conversation over afternoon tea had never happened before.

"We are definitely an unusual family!"

Anna is the next with a question. "Can you chose the exact moment to leave?"

"Yes, Anna. I can choose the out-breath that will be my last and simply shift out of existence in this physical world. From that moment, I will cease to be Jiang Cheng. Well, Jiang has already left. As you might know, I'll not go anywhere, because consciousness is not a thing, but is both infinite and takes up no space at the same time. My awareness will not be on the planet and nor will it be with you. Don't take it ill, but I must not mingle in your lives and you should not draw my attention here."

Ju-long has an appropriate question from a Chinese perspective. "So, we shouldn't make an altar for you?"

"Please, Ju-long. When you think of it, it wouldn't even make sense. Am I right?"

"You're right. What would be the deeper reason, anyway?"

Mum looks at her mum. "Even if you reincarnated, the altar wouldn't have any deeper meaning for you, as Ju-long said. It might have some meaning for the ones still here. I'm not talking about us, but people in general."

Dad comments on both his wife and his mother-in-law. "The one who leaves should not constantly be reminded by the ones the person has left. There must be other tasks at hand for the one who left to focus on."

I feel it is time to shift the focus now. "So a release and good journey party would be appropriate."

Grandma smiles. "Yes, a celebration in joy, like the joy I Am feeling over beginning a new journey. Let's do it tomorrow."

After this, we make a rough plan to be carried out tomorrow. Kong, who had been silent during this conversation, suggests he and Julia make the decorations. He has brought some materials for Julia and whoever wants to join in.

What could have been a serious or sad evening becomes one of joy and anticipation for the time to come. There is still time for some shopping, and later Cheng drives Grandma back to her home while Kong prefers to walk to his. As he says, "The evening chill makes me feel alive, and that is exactly what everyone should feel on the planet. This feeling becomes a sensation from deep inside of the fact that I exist!"

Knowing Kong's past, it is wonderful to hear. Becoming a grandpa for the second time with Li — well, kind of — must have boosted his joyful feeling.

The next morning, which is November 11, at breakfast, Kong is back and tells us he had a wonderful meeting with Li in the night. He is reluctant to talk about it.

"I really can't express the sensations in words, because they are not of this world. The description will be pretty flat compared to the actual event."

Ju-long comments on his dad's reluctance. "We totally relate to that. It's a personal experience that will only degrade if told in human words."

Grandma Jiang has chosen noon today as the time for the main festivity for her departure.

"It will be when the sun is at its highest on the arc of its path. Yet the point of the arc is, as we know, an illusion, because the star travels through space in a spiral motion, always traversing new areas."

We are up early. There are foods that take time to prepare and we are all busy, but in a good way. It is like when Anna and I were young, living with our parents in Hong Kong; all join the preparation of the meal.

I am with Julia and Kong at the dining table making place cards, which Julia always does to such events. I enjoy spending time with Kong. He still makes his artwork, different kinds of paintings, jewellery and wood-carved pictures with inlays of different colours of wood and other materials, and usually black lines of ink where suitable. He has brought his latest work to show me. It's a set of Mah-jong tiles, where he, besides the normal colours in ink and paint, has used some gold paint. The tiles look exclusive.

Dad and Cheng are out shopping. The rest are in the kitchen and we can easily hear them from where we sit.

Anna starts a new dialogue. "Grandma, you look and behave younger than I can remember since I became an adult."

"As I said yesterday, the human I is now a facet of ME, so it's ME you see shining through the human guise. My infinity-train will stop at 'Planet Earth' this last time and pick me up, and I'm so excited to get on board. That's what you experience."

Mum joins in. "One can often see this deep connection shortly before a person dies, and this is actually what happens here, right?"

"Indeed, death is beautiful and so easy if you can let go of the life that has ended. One must celebrate and honour the person for the journey without judgement."

Ju-long turns to Grandma. "Jiang, I remember this happened with your late husband."

"Yes. At that time, I saw it as he came back for the last goodbye. Now I know it was much more HIM than Cheng that showed up."

Anna gets an inner picture of ascending.

"See you later in the elevator!" Ju-long's tone tells me he is teasing her.

"You're so good with lyrics. It rhymes and all!"

"Well, it's the elevator to Heaven, but I can't find a good rhyme that will work!"

Back at the dinner table with Julia and Kong, Julia paints all the place cards with a background of water colours. She explains who will have the card with the specific background, and then Kong makes a small motif. Lastly, I write the name of the person. We use a small fan so the paint dries quickly between each step.

After finishing the place cards, it is only natural that Julia and Kong set the dinner table, assisted by Ting. The grandparents, with their first grandchild, are all into the interaction with the small girl, and the long separation between the two adults and Ting's new husband are just events among many others in one of many lives. These are my thoughts mixed with Julia's comment at the moment I observe them interacting.

Grandma and Kong have been working on something too. Grandma has written a letter to each of us about our relation with her during the time we have known her in this lifetime. When we are all dressed up for the meal, she asks us to gather in the living room around the low table where she hands a letter to everyone. She has completed the letter with some wise words to go with our lives in the experiences to come. They are beautifully handwritten and signed with a wavey blue line, symbolising a river, her name in Chinese. She had asked Kong to make an illustration after her description of each of them, without him knowing the contents.

Anna asks her grandma, "So, did Kong make his own illustration?"

"Oh, I asked your mother to do that one, dear Anna. And I must say, she did a pretty good job!"

Below is a list of the illustrations, all with a title note.

Her great granddaughter, Julia: The little giant. You sing your song and move the planet.

Picture: A breeze moves some rushes or papyrus and ripples a water surface.

Her youngest grandchild, Anna: Singing the child awake. Bringing joy and spontaneity into the life of people.

Picture: A young child in rubber boots playing with a paper boat in a small pond.

Her eldest grandchild, Luzi: Light, feminine, star of Stars.

Picture: A sun with a halo.

Her daughter, Ya: The yellow morning sun, always rising to its full glory.

Picture: A sun rises over misty scenery.

Her son-in-law, Carl: The wise of the wise. The ocean deep seems black and empty, but its wisdom will surface.

Picture: A dolphin jumps out of the water.

Her grandson-in-law, Ju-long: The knight pursues.

Picture: A wanderer with a staff on his way up a steep mountain trail.

Ju-long's mother, Ting: The crystal water reflecting the blue sky.

Picture: Some still water reflects the clouds and the surrounding landscape.

Ting's new husband, Cheng: Kindness in all matters. Feeding the sparrow and stroking the dragon.

Picture: A sparrow on the ground to the left, a dragon's head to the right facing left. A kneeling person in the middle, seen from the back, with the left hand down to the bird and the right hand up to the dragon's face.

Ju-long's father, Kong: Not a cloud in sight. Looking at a clear blue sky, we can't see the depth and the vastness, but we know it is there.

Picture: A blue sky turning into an ocean with a single traditional Chinese fishing boat.

Grandma reads the letter to her great grandchild, so they share it on a human level, but I know they have communication on other levels as well.

The rest of us save the letter for an appropriate time.

The "transition" meal is as cheerful as any anniversary meal. We take the time to enjoy the foods prepared by ourselves in love to life, and it seems that this love to life is the main theme in the stories we share around the table.

After the mail and a quick clean-up, we have tea in Ting and Chang's beautiful garden.

Before we left Hastings, Ju-long scanned and sent the stylistic watercolour painting Julia made of Grandma in a very high resolution to Kong here in Hong Kong. He then arranged for a print in a large format, 70 x 150 cm (28 x 59 inch), on water-proof art silk fabric as a gift for Mum. *See the painting in the chapter, "Spring", subchapter, "Mum and Dad visit".*

Grandma comments on the gift. "I know I'm your human mother and I birthed your biological body, but we are not our bodies, we are US. So a picture on the wall or in your mind of this human body, young or old, will not represent ME. Julia's painting, with its simplicity, is much more suitable."

Anna has a proposal for her grandmother. "Grandma, how about tomorrow we visit some places you and Grandpa took us when Luzi and I were children?"

"Oh, Anna, it is old connections for what seems ages ago. You can always visit the places, but you'll only meet your old self and the grandparents we were at that time. Visit new and wonderful places when you feel ready for it, just as I'm going to do!"

There is a great truth in these wise words. You CAN visit old places from way back in your life and even lives, and you will find that there is not much to the places, and all you can do is let it all go. What seems important or huge at the time has mostly been transmuted to wisdom, and only the human understanding of it remains as an empty shell of the REAL beauty in the experience without human judgement.

Anna comes with her next question, which is the one we all would like to get answered. "When will you board the train? While we are here now?"

"I'll hand in my ticket when you are back home and in a moment of my choosing, but don't count me in for the Christmas celebrations. I'll swing by each of you for a last hug, and then I'll be on my way!"

I can clearly sense her anticipation, and I know it is what makes her seem so alive and vibrant.

In the evening Dad buys Kong's mah-jong tiles, because he and Mum have many business relations to whom they give unique gifts upon visits. Dad is generous with the payment and he has talked with Kong about the necessity of energy exchange. Earlier, Kong had some difficulties accepting a high price for his unique creations, but it seems to work fine now. Dad knows how much work Kong has put into the work, and he doesn't want to get the beautiful work for a bargain price.

In the following days, Grandma is so much alive and back to her "old" self that I wish she could stay, watching her grandchildren growing up. It is almost like seeing her when Anna and I were kids.

It is difficult for us to leave this old woman, and Ting, Mum, Anna and I are all tears when we say our last goodbye. It would somehow have been easier if she was a sick and dying human being. What helps us is that we know that this woman is just a minute part of what she really is. Julia, on the other hand, is as joyful as ever, joining the celebration of the true departure.

She explains it to me. "It's not sadness you feel. It's the true sense of love bouncing back and forth between all of us."

I do my best to stay in the feeling, even though it is nearly unbearable.

Julia continues. "Dive or relax into this sense rather than fighting it. You eventually must get used to it, anyway."

I would like to ask what she means, but it must wait until a better time. My mind seems to have shut down for the time being.

I can't read the letter from Grandma until we are back in Hastings. I sit near the lit wood burner with my legs pulled up, but feel a chill inside me. The slippers and the thick blanket don't seem to help much. I am alone in the house except for the cats, which lie on a blanket near the wood burner. I am a little sad, and this may be a good time to read the letter. After a sip of my hot tea, I pull out the handwritten pages with Kong's painting of the Sun with a halo on top. The text below it says, *Light*, *feminine, star of Stars.* Immediately the connection is there and I turn to the next page.

Dear, YOU.

I am with you in these moments while you read this letter and there is no time between the writing and the reading nor is there between you and me. The sadness you feel is not because you feel you'll lose me, your grandmother; you're not Lucia and I'm not Grandma. Letting go of so much of what you thought you were, in ALL lifetimes even before incarnating the first time, brings forth the sadness. Letting go of a grandmother being just one of them. I, as your grandmother, went through the same experiences. I didn't share them with you, because they are so personal and I want you to focus on YOUR own letting go and your own discovery of YOU. And indeed that will be great in an almost terrifying way; meeting your own grandness!

Speaking of your future makes no sense in the respect that there is none. You are the ocean in which you dive. That is what it really means when we say there is no separation. You're not separate from you! This is the true oneness. One with God if you like; you with you. This is the love Julia talked about when we said our human goodbyes.

Be in joy on your journey,
The River of Me.

In the evening, in bed, I share my letter with Julong. I do this because I feel, even though the letter is highly personal, we walk our paths together. I get a picture of he and I holding hands while walking on a gravel road, each in our own wheel track.

I, already in bed, see Ju-long has his letter in hand when he comes to bed. He also wants to share it with me.

In his picture, the wanderer with the staff on his way corresponds with my picture of the gravel road and our journey. He will never give up and my light will always shine.

Dear, YOU.

From a life with straitened circumstances you have given yourself the opportunity of expansion, and now you're well underway. You've realised there is so much more to life than you've previously known, and you are only into the beginning. When you dance with the rest of your new family, you're shown there are no limits to what you can become, and that it all comes down to simply allowing.

So dance away my dear,
The River of Me

I had no idea when Grandma would embark on her next grand journey, but one sunny afternoon still in November, when Julia and I are in the garden, dressed warm because the air is cold and damp, I sense the smell of Grandma so clearly as if she stands right next to me.

"And I Am right next to you; in human terms, anyway. My ticket has just been stamped, by myself of course, and I'm here for the final let go."

I feel a physical hug, and at the same time Julia laughs out loud in joy.

"Bye Granny!"

I am all tears. Julia comes up to me, I kneel and we hug for a while … all three of us.

Soul destiny

After Grandma's unique departure, I talk with Sekhmet about stuff we have touched on from time to time. Just to clarify that when we use the term soul, it is NOT the soul in the God-Soul-Human hierarchy. There CAN be no hierarchy here. One more statement, this one from Saint Germain: the Soul Destiny is the only destiny there is.

Sekhmet wants me to shift from being the one who asks the questions to be together with her answering them before my human part even asks them.

"You're not less wise than I, and there is no hierarchy, as it has just being stated!"

So here we go as a collective writer.

What the human belief system calls the soul is the Master Wisdom built of the wisdom derived from all lifetimes. When enlightenment or realisation occurs, the soul or Master Wisdom is woven into the fabric of the I Am, and the Gnost will be the primary wisdom in the life. The human persona will likewise be woven in as yet another facet, like all the other human lifetimes, this being just one of many. This will make the total of the I Am THAT, where THAT is "added" to the I Am. The body will become a free-energy vessel. The destiny of the soul or the Master Wisdom is the integration into the I Am, being part of THAT. After this, any experience through an embodied realised being will not need to be turned into wisdom, because the experience happens "inside" THAT. There is NO OUTSIDE! Consciousness and infinite New Energy are not two separate things. They are inseparable parts of THAT. I remember Saint Germain's BON screen where ALL experience happens. So, no outside.

The human mind experiences the world as being outside itself, because both are "in" the BON, like side by side, so they can play.

When you wake up after being in a dream where you fell, you are yourself in the dream world; you know you were in a dream. The dream represents the BON. Sometimes you know in the dream you are dreaming. This is the AND. But remember, there are or can be many ANDs.

Allow free, original energy from The One's burst of expression to work with the I Am. This free energy is non-biased and therefore different or acts differently from the energy used in duality.

Could the mind use this free energy and start a new paradigm of humanity?

Yes, the neurons will chance and some will be replaced so they can communicate with the new or free energy.

Can we have a humanity on Earth WITHOUT DUALITY?

No, humanity IS duality. But people who choose to move from a life of FOCUS on the old duality can live in the AND so that duality becomes an option one can switch in and out of. One must be able to recognise the AND before one can choose it. That, in a sense, is the brilliance of it. Two people living together can have totally different lives, solely because of how they perceive their own life.

So, what the human can do, because the mind ALWAYS wants to DO things, is as stated: Allow your soul destiny.

I remember Saint Germain says it this way:

"It is up to the human to say: I'm done with this human merry-go-round! You must REALLY want this and be willing to die to do it; and you must; your human ego, anyway. But the human is in its own way most of the time, thinking there is something it must do to go into realisation. The human gets distracted by all the things which don't work out most of the time because of the Master disrupting it. This includes killing itself."

Because the person can't jump off the merry-go-round and let go of what makes this person in all its unperfect perfection, the Master steps in. What the person CAN do is allow the process. Saint Germain calls it allowing YOU, which is ALL you are. We call it I Am THAT.

Humans are true space travellers

In these, in every way, exciting times, my awareness is much into what will come. To me, it is very much about what and how my two children will contribute to it. Julia is under two years old, but the consciousness she is, is well underway with those things. I expect no less from Li, whom I look forward to meeting in person.

Sekhmet and my conversation takes another route.

The AI will take us to the stars, as Saint Germain said earlier in this book, and to this Sekhmet adds a comment.

"You live in space. You live amongst the stars. The closest one is the sun! The Earth moves through space at a speed of 390 km per second towards the constellation Leo, the Lion, which is in our own galaxy. Our galaxy moves through space at an even faster speed."

I realise what she says is true. Earth is our space ship on autopilot. Later, I found these figures: If you stand on the surface of the Earth at the equator, you move at 460 metres per second. This is the speed of the planet's spin around its axis. The Earth moves around the sun at a speed of nearly 30 km per second or 67,000 miles per hour. The solar system moves around the centre of our galaxy at 220 km per second or 490,000 miles per hour. Our galaxy, The Milky Way, moves through space with a speed of nearly 1,000 km per second. This really gets me in awe.

"So, every object in space moves around something and that something moves too. This means that everything moves in spirals, even the spirals. The Earth moves in the spiral that the Sun creates and that spiral moves in yet another spiral that the Milky Way creates by its movement through space.

We always pass through a new part of space every second, never the same spot! This sets the twenty-four-hour cycle in perspective! It is much more than just a new day; it is a new space as well!"

Sekhmet explains why humanity wants Artificial Intelligence. I hope we will find a new term for AI soon, because the term we use right now really doesn't fit.

"So, you see, dear Luzi, humanity must have the AI to bring them to the stars. You can't just plot a linear course from A to B because every part of space moves in spirals, and it takes immense calculation power to navigate in that vast space."

"I see. We need the AI to write the programs that then do the calculations and readjustments."

"You can't separate AI as a concept from the programmer, the programme and the hardware. And consciousness or awareness IS part of it too."

I sense she has a conversation with someone, or maybe it is a part of herself she communicates with, so I wait for her to return to me.

She continues. "A fully realised and embodied person will not use a spaceship of any kind to travel from planet Earth to any part of the cosmos, because there is no need to move the human body. If you wish to appear with a body, you simply create one, maybe using the blueprint of your human body."

"That is so cool. I can simply 'warp' to a planet, for

example around Alpha Centauri, in an instant!"

Sekhmet smiles. "And you don't have to use any AI or even the human brain to get there. You would have arrived before the human had finished the thought of taking the trip."

I have also been thinking how the human body will change.

There are various traces of Neanderthals and Denisovans in the DNA of modern *Homo sapiens sapiens*. These hominids are now extinct, but live on in today's humans. They may even be the reason we, the *Homo sapiens*, have become so successful quantity-wise; we have adapted some details that, in combination, gave us some advantages. In the future, the new humans, built with the help of "AI", may have only traces of the *Homo sapiens* genetic makeup in their bodies.

Christmas 2020

We begin this December much like we did the previous one. We have finally completed the changes of the dome house, and we look forward to spending another Christmas Eve in our new home. This time we only have my parents and Anna on visit, but we have new arrivals in the flock to compensate for that. Jack, Blue and Snow are the newcomers, who bring life and joy into our home.

Dad has offered Kong a plane ticket so he can be with his granddaughter this Christmas as Dad did last year for him and Grandma. Kong has turned down the offer, or rather asked Dad if he could postpone the visit till August, when Li is supposed to arrive. Dad replied that he would offer Kong tickets for both occasions.

Kong declined and explained that one trip a year was what he could accept. Seen with an average person's eyes, I understand Kong. Even an economy-class return ticket Hong Kong–London is expensive, and Dad would never go for less than business class; first class if possible. This is simply the way things are. Kong needs to keep even a minimum of energetic balance between him and Dad. I hope that Kong will someday see that this is not the way real energy balance works.

While this runs through my mind, Julia pops in with a comment. I am in the kitchen and she sits under the tree in the living room with the birds. I get a glimpse of her face with a big smile when we make eye contact. We wave at each other. She communicates non-verbally.

"You know there really is no such thing as energy balance between any two individuals, but there is a system of energy flow allowance in a person's energy. And this is even not the whole or real truth, if one can say that."

"So if I give or pay for something, I feel I am worthy to receive that something. It's really not about energy, but worthiness."

"Right, Luzi. If the person doesn't feel worthy, being aware of this or not, it limits the flow of energy in that person's life."

"But what if I bargain to get something cheap?"

"Then it's the lack-thing playing out, and that surely turns down the energy flow!"

"So I shouldn't bargain?"

"That totally depends on the situation. If it is a tradition to bargain and you know what's going on, then it's fine, energy wise."

"So if I bargain with focus on getting as much for as little as possible, the energy tab turns down, but if the price is set high for a bargain to take place it's OK."

"In the end, it doesn't matter. It's all just a game, right?!"

Julia hasn't stopped talking and playing with Blue during our conversation. She looks just like any other small child with her focus on the play. I can hear she really puts the bird to the test. They are playing with shapes and colours at the same time, and Blue also practises his speech.

"Now, Blue, give me a green cube."

"Green cube."

I ask Isis if she takes part in the play.

"Oh, hi Luzi. What?"

I smile. "Obviously not."

"Well, no. I don't have the slightest idea of what they are doing. You can't expect me to play parrot all the time!"

We both laugh. I like Isis best when she plays off with some personality.

"You can go back to your coloured magazine and your nail file, Isis!"

"Don't forget the long drink … -s, dear!"

And off she went.

"Well played!"

Imagine Isis turning her head on her way out: "Always, dear, always!"

We laugh.

Luzi's thirty-first birthday

Having a birthday on 20 December may be troublesome for some because they feel they must turn their imagination into mash to find a gift for my birthday and Christmas too. The brilliant solution is that people can choose a gift for ONE of the events. It was not so important in Hong Kong, because we didn't expect the presents to be expensive. Often a beautiful card, mostly with some personal words from the giver, would do.

It is Sunday morning. Last night, just before we went to bed, Ju-long casually told me that if I heard some moving around in the kitchen very early the next morning, he would take care of it, so I could continue my sleep. I get the hint. He and Julia have a plan. Most likely breakfast in bed.

I wake up at 5:14, and instead of going back to sleep, I sneak into the bathroom to pee. This so I don't have to get up to pee later with a salver over my legs and a bed full of people and probably animals too.

Sure enough. At 6 a.m. Ju-long kisses me and sneaks out into the bathroom. Shortly after, I hear a whisper in the centre area and then some commotion in the kitchen. I turn to lie on my back, pull up the blanket to my chin and wait for the surprise.

I had actually fallen asleep and wake up when I hear them sneaking at the bedroom door. The tea trolley rolls in with sparklers lit while Julia and Ju-long sing a birthday song for me. It is very touching, especially seeing Julia, that little girl of only one year and seven months, being so excited, singing with such a clear voice.

"Happy birthday, Mum!"

"Happy birthday, dear Luzi!"

Ju-long makes a little more light in the room and places a bed salver over my legs. They set the "table" for all three of us, keeping most on the tea trolley. I see there are treats for the animals, and loud meows tells us the cats are soon be in the bed too. After saying good morning to Snow and Boomer, Ju-long shows them the treats in the bowls on the floor next to the bed.

Flapping wings tell us that the birds won't let us party without them. They land on the foot of the bed and Julia gives them their cue.

"Happy birthday, Luzi."

Both birds repeat it with their bird voices, but flawless in their expression. I open my arms wide and invite the birds for a hug.

"Thank you, Jack and Blue. Come here for a big morning hug!"

Ju-long moves the bed salver a little so I can turn to the right to receive the birds. It is the side Julia is on, so she moves away too. After the hug, Julia points at the bowls on the floor next to her father's side of the bed.

"Birds, go for the treats!"

There is a little confusion, because the salver is in the way, but they manage to jump off the bed towards the food and walk over next to the cats. The treats are soon dealt with, and our furred and feathered family members join us in the bed. They are not begging for treats, but lie or sit near or up against us.

My daughter is eager to begin. "There are presents for you, Mum. This one is from me and Sarah!"

She hands me the first one. It is wrapped in Christmas wrapping paper and a curling ribbon, about four centimetres square and half of a centimetre thick. It is a little heavy for the size, and flexible.

I open it and find a square image made of tiny glass beads bound by string. It looks abstract, but Julia gives a little help.

"Yes, that's up. It is a picture of a place. One you know!"

I squint, but with no success.

Ju-long has the solution.

"Stretch you arm, then the spaces between the beads will diminish."

"Wow, now it's very clear. It's Elvendale City, seen from the grasslands, showing the bridge to the left, the city to the right and a bit of the lake at the bottom. It's beautiful. Thank you, dear!"

I am impressed and so is Ju-long.

"Did you make this all by yourself?"

"I chose the colours and Sarah helped with the string."

Later, I count the beads. There are 48 by 48, which gives 2,304 in total! It has been quite a job for the two girls to undertake.

The proud father has a technical question. "How could you even construct the picture? I mean, you must divide it up in little pieces."

"I had the city in front of me and held up a net of imaginary clear glass beads. Then I just had to tell Sarah which bead to pick, one at the time."

She hands me the next present. It is the size of a jewellery box. It has the same kind of wrapping and ribbon as the first one.

"This is from all of us, here and in Hong Kong."

It is an all-jade ring. Almost transparent green, as if smoke is trapped inside. I hold it up to the light and look into it.

"Oh, it's so beautiful! Come get a hug, Julia!"

We are careful not to shuffle the salver. Also Ju-long reach over and gives me a hug with one arm and his cheek to mine. I sense his feelings, which could translate to the human words for a deep joy and satisfaction with life. In short, I would call it grateful to life.

I put on the ring and hold it up in front of the light again. Julia grabs my hand and pulls it over in front of my eyes and turns it towards the light.

"There really is smoke inside!"

We continue with the lovely breakfast. The birds leave us after a while, while the cats curls up, almost on top of each other, taking another nap.

Christmas Day

Let us jump to Christmas Day 25 December. We continue our Chinese/British tradition with Julong's and my twist.

We have no Christmas tree, and I understand most of the other villagers don't either. Some have a fir growing in a large flowerpot, but without heavy decorations. Like last year, we have a large kissing bough with electrical candles hanging from the ceiling in the living room.

Anna has helped Mum and Dad in Sevenoaks to prepare some food, so when they arrive in the morning, Dad walks up to the house with two large boxes, which he can hardly look over.

"I'm so hungry after having smelled the food all the way!"

Anna is there to support him.

"It was sheer torture … and for one entire hour! Man, that was hard."

Ju-long, still wearing his apron, and Julia go outside to help. Ju-long has been quick to dress her in her snowsuit and boots. Julia and Mum return with something that is obviously a surprise for later. They are very secretive about it. I stay in the kitchen to finish up SOMETHING. I would only be in the way while they carry all kinds of stuff inside, but I greet them as they come in. Boxes and bags keep coming in, and I wonder if the Tesla S has a trailer hooked on.

There are three rooms upstairs, one of them larger than the others, and two bathrooms. Mum and Dad get the large room and Anne one of the small ones. This will be our new study when Li moves in, taking over the present study on the ground floor. I like that we can invite people to stay overnight without having them in the living room.

At last it is time for a proper hello and the sharing of hugs, and Anna is the first in line.

"Lovely to see you again, sis. It's been a while since your last visit!"

"Sis, you too! We can't all live in the south by the sea. When more palm trees show up along the shore, forming nice alleys, I may consider getting a comfortable bamboo cabin at the beach!"

"Then this igloo will seem out of place, for sure!"

"But you can just overgrow it with plants, and it

will be a perfect Hobbit house instead!"

"Oh, Anna, your imagination never fails!"

"I know, I'm good … Well, even magnificent and adorable!"

Julia comes up to us already wearing a new dress, which I guess she will wear at the Christmas dinner. It is a A-line dress with semi-long sleeves in Scotch colours on a red base and with large, white snowflakes at the bottom.

"Yes, Auntie Anna. You are THE BEST!"

Anna crouches down to her admirer and hugs the small girl.

"That's because I'm the ONLY auntie you have! Right?"

Julia looks her straight in the eyes with a serious face. "You are a sly fox, too. Did you know that?" Now she laughs and gives Anna another hug.

"And you are a cunning niece, so beautiful in your new dress. It's from Grandma Ya, I guess!"

"And Grandpa."

Mum shows up after her visit to the bathroom. "Actually, it was Carl who chose it out of three I had picked."

Mum and I hug, and she whispers in my ear. "She is so adorable and could make me cry all the time, if I didn't hold back."

I whisper back. "Then think of me. I'm with her all the time!"

"Poor you!"

We let go, and Dad comes up for a hug too. "Merry Christmas, dear. It feels good to be here!"

"And merry Christmas to you, Dad. It's good to have you all here again. Last Christmas seems to have happened just a few days back, but at the same time it was eons ago."

"When a lot happens, it stretches time, and events seem to have taken place long ago."

Ju-long joins us with two plates of food for the table. "I heard someone talking about being hungry, and is there a young woman almost starved to death? Give me a hand everyone, and we'll have brunch in no time."

Anna and Julia run to the kitchen, sounding like a bunch of wild warriors in full pursuit.

Julia shows us the full meaning of living in the AND. She comments on a picture I have of the consciousness sitting INSIDE the small body, controlling it as if she is inside a robot.

"Stop that, silly you! I AM the one-and-a-half-year-old Julia AND I am ME."

"Yes, silly of me. Sorry!"

"Don't feel sorry, just be silly like the rest of us, including Anna!"

Yes, blessed be Anna, so spontaneous.

Soon after, we are all sitting at the table enjoying the food and the company. We can't be sitting here all day, though. There is still food to prepare and arrange, and I know Julia will make some last-minute Christmas decorations together with whoever wants to take part. Oh, and place cards too. Mum will be a part of it for sure.

In the end each of us spends time with Julia at the low table in the living room. This year the living room looks different from last year. Now we have a huge tree up the outer wall. At the centre area of the house and partly the back of the living room, an elegant concrete staircase leads up to a gallery on the second floor. The elevator hides in the shadows in the back of the centre area.

We sit down for the Christmas dinner close to 1:30 p.m., all dressed up in our best clothes. Last year Julia was barefoot, but this time she wears white socks and white shoes.

"Like the snow on my dress!"

Dad turns to her. "Is there a fine place around here to run a toboggan down a hill?"

"Yes, and it's good for a butt slide too!"

We all laugh.

"Yes, Dad. There's a small hill at the other side of Barley Lane."

Ju-long, who finds the hill on the small side of too little, as Tigger may say, comes up with an alternative. "But the best place is East Hill, two kilometres from here."

I must caution, because I know East Hill. "There is a less steep place just before East Hill, behind the Rocklands Holiday Park. You can find it by turning left when you come to East Hill."

Dad puts on a big smile. "So, that could be a good place to bring hot cocoa, rolls, and, of course, our butts?"

Julia is very excited. "Yes, we'll go butt sliding in the snow!"

Anna raises a hand and waves it. "Me too, me too!"

Julia turns to Anna, frowning. "Aunty, have you brought your butt?" Then she laughs.

"Always! One never knows when one might need it!"

Mum, being practical, puts a lid on the excitement. "It will be too late today. It will soon be dark, but tomorrow will be fine, especially if the Sun shines."

Julia turns to her grandma with a put-on reproachful face. "Butt, Grandma?!" Then she laughs again.

Inside the igloo, we have the most joyful and warm Christmas Day. The wood burner is on and adds to the atmosphere.

The cats love the attention from our guests, being brushed and stroked, but the birds want to be more active and they play different games, including Julia's form-and-colour game.

Oh, and not to forget the surprise from Julia and Mum. They have brought a series of jigsaw puzzles for Christmas, each with a motif of one of the family members, including the three in Hong Kong and the non-humans. There is some space between the tiles, so the birds' claws can pick a tile up again if it doesn't quite fit. They have forty-eight to ninety-six pieces each. The number of pieces is Julia's choice.

"The birds are pretty smart, and it's OK if it's difficult at first. They have excellent memories, which helps them to do them faster with some training."

The next morning greets us with a clear, blue sky and therefore sunshine, calm and crisp air and creaking snow under our feet. After breakfast, we are all heading for East Hill. We have borrowed some toboggans, a bobsled, and a pan sled. Dad has borrowed Ju-long's rain pants, because, in Julia's opinion, using a pan sled is NOT butt sliding. Dad has only himself to blame if it hurts. Julia wears diapers and her white snowsuit.

The cats love the snow. They would usually sleep most of the day, but today, with only a little wind, they are out playing in this marvellous white world. The birds prefer to look at all this whiteness from above, sitting in the trees. Blue doesn't fly much being a hyacinth macaw and suited to much warmer climates. I guess Jack is built to handle the cold better. He sometimes takes off by himself, but is usually not gone for long. I am sure he prefers to share his adventures with Blue.

We arrive at the top of East Hill and turn left, following a path already trod, until we walk through a tree line to find ourselves at the top of a perfect sliding hill.

Dad and Julia are the first to sit down at the start of a pathway of compressed snow leading down the hill in an almost straight line.

As they are halfway down the path, I remember something Julia told me non-verbally when her body was three months old. She talked about the past/future subject which the mind needs.

"I remember from my future as Julia, being only a few years old, that Grandad Carl and I are out in the snow. I'm dressed in a white suit. We are sitting on the top of a hill; someone has already laid out the slide path. We hold hands, my right in Carl's left. Now we slide down the hill on our butts. It's so thrilling. I feel Carl's joy, and my thrilling mixes in a beautiful dance of 'I exist'."

This future event also gave baby Julia her name for Dad, Wuuw, the sound you cry out when you slide down a snow-covered hill on your butt.

THE END

I find this is a suitable spot to break the story. It will continue in the beginning of 2021, the year when William Li Wang will appear on the planet. I am so looking forward to finding out how it all plays out!

I hope you have enjoyed the book and ask you to take a moment to make a brief review on your favourite retailer website, or send it to me.

Thanks in advance, Eriqa Queen.

Author's comments

Writing this fourth book has differed from the others. A lot of detail came in at the same time. Like a pile of stepping stones, I had to lay them out to get a natural flow in the story, writing them one at the time from the pile.

This time, the story has brought me quite a few surprises. I am the writer or typist more than an author, as if the story or the characters orchestrate the action themselves. Thank you for that. It is always exciting to stand in the middle of the action without a clue what will happen, and being surprised that the action goes THAT way! Even Jack the raven told me how he would drink a small amount of cream from a saucer by turning his head to the side and licking it up.

And this scene at Christmas: "Julia and Mum return with something that is obviously a surprise for later. They are very secretive about it." I had no idea what it was, but I sensed a broad smile from Julia. I had to wait until the story revealed it to me.

Also, this time while writing I shed a lot of joyful tears as I connected with these wonderful beings who make up the gallery of the story.

I have read through the text several times and it strikes me how much I have learned during the period of writing this particular book. Now I feel I was almost naïve in the beginning, growing more mature during the composition of the text and underlying energies while working with everyone involved.

As you have read the book, you might have noticed repeated information, maybe in slightly different ways both from the previous books and this one. We have done this to make it more adaptable for the mind. The coherence may be lost if we present only the new information.

I will publish two more titles in this series. After that, on request from Julia, we plan an additional series featuring Julia as the storyteller and protagonist, following her life in four titles.

Additions

These additions continue the list from the previous books. There is so much material that in different ways can trigger your depths and make you remember, so this list is just some small examples related to the content of the book.

Music

"Someday", Roxanne – Texas singer & songwriter, (Roxanne Anderson), https://www.reverbnation.com/roxannerox.

"The Sound of Silence", Paul Simon.

I rarely comment on lyrics. I want you to sense into it yourself. But this song is so often misunderstood when someone says it is about people not committing in their conversations with others. So WHY is it that people don't really speak who they are and listen in a dialogue?

The OUTSIDE silence of NOT communicating happens because we seek a much deeper and fulfilling dialogue, a dialogue which we may have forgotten, but still feel in a way. It is something we can't get from anyone outside of ourselves.

Paul's old friend the darkness is the I Am, always willing to LISTEN if you are willing to SPEAK, maybe not in words, but in senses … in the sound of silence. In the silence you can sense the I Am, which will always listen to your tales from the outside world or whatever you want to share.

Films

Citizen Bio, (2020).

David Attenborough: A Life on Our Planet, (2020). (9.2/10 on IMDb). This movie lines up with what Julia works with.

Ghost in the Shell, (1995), *Innocence* (2004), *Arise Border – Ghost Tears* (2014), *Arise Border – Ghost Stands Alone* (2014). All cartoons.

Ghost in the Shell, (2017), live actors.

Interreflections, (2020), director & writer: Peter Joseph.

Westworld, TV series (2016–).

Books

Do You Speak Future? Book of Insights, (2020), Jacque Fresco, ISBN 9780964880634. Check the "Store" at www.thevenusproject.com for his free stream, "Jacque Fresco - Machine Government".

Journey of Souls, (2005) (5. edition), Michael Newton, ISBN 978-1-56718-485-3.

Journey of the Angels, (2019), Geoffrey Hoppe, ISBN 978-1712672990 & Kindle ASIN B0837TR7RR.

There's No Such Place As Far Away, (1993), Richard Bach, ISBN 0-00-647730-5.

America Before: The Key to Earth's Lost Civilization, (2019), Graham Hancock, http://grahamhancock.com/america-before/

Links

Links, especially to YouTube, may not work for various reasons. You may find the materials if you search the titles inside or outside of YouTube.

This is a video I found after writing about the Black Soil in South America (see from 46:00-47:30 minutes): *America Before: The Key to Earth's Lost Civilisation*, by Graham Hancock. This is also the title of one of his books: https://youtu.be/GAc-cZ8eWhXo

The Venus Project: https://www.thevenusproject.com/

HIDDEN TEACHINGS of the Bible That Explain Manifestation, Consciousness & Oneness: https://youtu.be/_ZQ03ki7-UU

Hong Kong vs. China: https://www.investopedia.com/articles/investing/121814/hong-kong-vs-china-understand-differences.asp

"No single birthplace of mankind, say scientists."
Article in *The Guardian*: https://www.theguardian.com/science/2018/jul/11/no-single-birthplace-of-mankind-say-scientists

Terra preta, the black soil of the Amazonas by Antoinette M.G.A. WinklerPrins:
https://pdfs.semanticscholar.org/1d8d/a796a7c-cacea70e05f6251dbe131ca238337.pdf

Biochar: https://organicforecast.org/2018/02/bio-char-hearing-much/

The difference between organic and ecological farming:
https://www.baconline.co.uk/knowledge-centre/blog/3776-what-is-the-difference-between-organic-and-ecological-farming

https://www.biodynamics.com/biodynamic-principles-and-practices

Wakehurst: https://www.kew.org/Wakehurst

Excursions summer 2020
LEGOLAND Winsor Resort: www.legoland.co.uk
Little Street: www.little-street.co.uk
Brighton, British Air Ways tower: https://britishairwaysi360.com
Brighton, Sea Life: www.visitsealife.com/brighton/

Lightning Source UK Ltd.
Milton Keynes UK
UKHW010629301120
374362UK00001B/131